Lassoing Their Love

Doreen Milstead

Copyright © 2016 Doreen Milstead

All rights reserved.

ISBN: **1530372593**
ISBN-13: **978-1530372591**

CONTENTS

Mail Order Bride: From Germany To The Valley Of Silver...Page 5

Mail Order Bride: From France To The Other Side Of Paradise...Page 54

Mail Order Bride: Three English Sisters, One Cowboy & The Navajo Nation...Page 93

Mail Order Bride: Three Sisters & Ships, Trains & Stagecoaches Out West...Page 138

Doreen Milstead

Mail Order Bride: From Germany To The Valley Of Silver

Synopsis: Mail Order Bride: From Germany To The Valley Of Silver - Two men in one small town, a bad boy and a rancher, send away for a mail order bride; the only problem is -- one woman arrives on the train a few weeks later. A rivalry develops between the younger and older man and the gorgeous, talented, and cultured mail order bride from Germany.

    The two men stepped onto the wooden planks of the sidewalk outside the storefront of 'Pretty Brides From Back East.' They glanced at each other briefly before going into the office, either looking for courage to do it or for a sign that the deal was off. It was 1871 and in the newly minted silver mining town of Marlboro Valley, Colorado, men outnumbered women ten to one. The two men were tired of being caught up in that depressing statistic.
    One of the suitors in search of a bride was a former outlaw with intensity and arrogance vibrating through his young body and fire blazing in his eyes. Cody Johnson was his name - a strapping young man

of twenty-two years who sported spiky black hair, dense brown eyes and a long black duster with silver studs that gave a person a whiff of sex and danger when he passed by.

The women in the town all found him extremely attractive - riveting was more like it. It didn't matter if they were married, spoken for or loose with their morals, women loved the looks of Cody Johnson. For the man, though, none of those women were suitable enough to become his bride.

The other bachelor was rancher Brigham Whitestar, known as Brig to his plentiful group of friends. Brig was thirty one years old with startlingly ice-blue eyes in a weathered face, dusty wheat-colored hair and clothes that fit the man - a silver studded leather vest, soft pants that showed plenty of wear and a chambray shirt opened down the chest just far enough to make a woman drool. He dressed that way because he was a cowboy rancher who rode his land every day and because he wanted to.

Brig was his own man in every way, and he was particular about his women, too. Which is why he was stepping onto that porch at the office of a mail order bride operation. His bride would be hand-picked. He wanted a woman to share his life, a woman who would provide companionship and who would easily and willingly fit into the little nooks and crannies of a cowboy rancher's life.

Silver mining what the root of the Marlboro Valley and silver jewelry was the keepsake of most of its citizens - a status symbol. Women loved the local jewelry made with precious stones such as amethysts or turquoise, a lot of which also came from the hills of the valley. At parties and dances, the soft amber light of lanterns glanced and sparked off the handmade jewelry like the stars in the sky that twinkled over these open-air events.

But, it's important to understand the real value of the silver ore and jewelry that seemed to just spring out of Marlboro Valley. It brought business there. Investors, silver craftsmen, buyers and residents who not only came to buy, but to build the town into an economically sound place for people to live and raise families. As the town's population grew, so did the need for more businesses, like grocers and tack shops and blacksmiths and, well, saloons.

Saloons meant drinking and card playing, and those fun pastimes meant women. But they weren't the marrying kind of women - just temporary relief to men who spent their days in the mines or on ranches or in the stores, working hard to make a living and build a life. Like all the other businesses, one need often creates another, thus the mail order bride office that had opened to fill the need for the marrying kind of women that several of the local men needed but couldn't find in the valley.

Though it appeared the two men had come together, that wasn't the case at all. Men were competitors when it came to marriage-suitable women due to the short supply. Even if it was a mail order bride, there was still a "get to her first" attitude that was pervasive.

Brig and Cody arrived at the doorway to the mail order bride agency at exactly the same moment. They looked at each other again and suddenly, Brig's hand grabbed the doorknob, turned it, and pushed inwards. Never one to be last, Cody attempted to walk through at the same time so they were both stuck in the doorway, trying to get to the man in the office as fast as humanly possible.

Cody cursed under his breath, as the married couple who were the proprietors of Pretty Brides Back East, looked up. Brig removed his hat immediately but Cody didn't. They hovered over the couple's desk like two skinny vultures, glaring at each other.

"May we help you, gentlemen?" the man asked.

"I'd like to see what women you have," Brig said softly.

The woman looked up at Cody. "You, sir...what may we help you with?"

"Uh...me too...same as him." He jerked a thumb at Brig. "I want a woman as well."

"Not the same one, I hope," the proprietor said, jokingly but seriously. "We're not that sort of agency."

Neither Brig nor Cody saw the humor in the attempted joke. The man quickly pulled out two chairs for his customers.

"Gentlemen," he began, sliding two large catalogues across the desk toward them, "browse through these. My wife and I will be happy to answer any questions you might have. When you've made your decision about a lady, just let us know and we'll help you finalize the transaction.

"You make it sound like we're here to buy farm supplies," Cody said, pulling one of the books to a spot in front of him. "I'm looking for a bride, not a plow."

"I'm sorry if it sounded that way," the man said. "I respect you gentlemen, the ladies we represent and the purpose of your business here. Please, look through these to see if you have any interest in a woman who seems suitable to be your wife. There are some excellent candidates on those pages."

"That sounds better," Cody said, opening the cover of the catalogue he had selected.

Brig looked over at his competitor, appreciating the way he had set the man straight. He hated for his purpose to be diminished to a shopping spree. It was much more important and serious to him - just like it appeared to be for the flashy cowboy that sat beside him.

"One question," Brig said. "What is the process from the point of selecting someone from this book?"

The man took on his best business face.

"We'll take a deposit from you and contact the lady or ladies you select - on your behalf, of course.

Both Cody and Brig poured through the books, reading page after page of biographies and facts about women who wanted to become a bride to a man who needed whatever she was offering in terms of a marriage. After several pages, it was obvious most of the women said the same things in terms of what they were in search of, the only major difference being their personal information and where they were now living.

As it turned out, both men selected women from another country. Their experience with women who had already arrived in the east, or who had been born there, probably influenced their decisions.

Cody found his woman first and showed the man the page he had selected. They moved to another desk where Cody filled out a form, paid a deposit and asked about how he might contact the woman directly.

"You can't," the man said. "We prefer that you wait until she arrives here to establish personal contact. Some of these women are leaving home as young ladies whose parents would forbid them doing so."

"They are coming here legally, though, aren't they? I don't want any trouble with the law."

"Oh most definitely they are legal, and of legal age to be married. We don't have any laws in Colorado regarding age yet, but there is a given age where it is morally appropriate."

"And what is that?" Cody asked, curious but not concerned.

"Eighteen. We don't have any women in those catalogues that are under the age of eighteen. Which happens to also be the legal age in most European countries where most of the ladies are coming from to America. You have nothing to worry about Mr…..ah…"

"Johnson," Cody filled in the blank with a little impatience at the man's lack of knowing his customer's name. "Fine. I just don't want to be involved in transporting women across the big pond only to find out its an illegal thing."

"Certainly, I can understand that," the man said, folding Cody's cash deposit and sticking it in his pants pocket. "Nothing to worry about, Mr. Johnson. We'll be in touch as soon as we hear something from this young lady.

Cody took another look at Brig as he went out the door. The other man was now pouring through the pages of the book where Cody had found a young woman who sounded perfect for him. There were no pictures, which concerned him. But, it also made it necessary to look at the qualities of the women, not just their looks, which he had heard, were the first thing about a woman that disappeared. He wanted a life companion, not a beauty queen. But, he also wanted her to bee presentable in looks.

Just as Brig took the book to the man at the other desk to pay his deposit and complete the paperwork for his mail order bride, out of the corner of his eye, he saw Cody reining back his stallion in preparation to leave town. Brig wondered what sort of woman that wild cowboy had picked, but he was really more concerned that his own choice would be the right one for him.

Back at his rather nice house, Cody poured himself a drink of whiskey, sat down at his kitchen table and contemplated what he had just done.

A bride by mail, he thought to himself. I would never in a million years have thought it necessary for me to resort to finding a wife from a catalog of women who are probably as desperate to come to America as I am to find a wife. I'm a decent looking man whose never had a problem finding women to date, why couldn't I find a woman to marry among the many who pass through the valley.

But Cody knew the answer to the question already. He was selective, no, picky. Cody Johnson was a picky man when it came to women who he would invest any personal time in - and that meant romance. He had never been in love in his life.

Brig felt excited about his success in locating a woman he thought would be perfect for him and his prospering cattle ranch. She seemed strong, determined and educated, a quality which was necessary for the well-read man. It wasn't enough to be a partner in sex and housekeeping, Brig wanted more.

He wanted a woman who could carry on an intelligent conversation, raise children and help him build his ranching empire that he had long envisioned to be his destiny. Politics were in the horizon of his mind's eye, so that meant that a lady on his arm had to look and act that part, too.

When Brig got back to his modest, one-bedroom home, he began laying out plans for how the house could be enlarged, what furniture and other appointments a woman might want and even to what patch of ground around the house would make the best flower garden. He knew enough about women to know they always wanted flowers.

In Bavaria, Greta Stein carefully selected the clothes that she would take with her to America. She knew nothing of the climate or the dressing habits of women in Colorado. Much less did she know about the man she had agreed to marry. He was her age, he owned a flourishing ranch and he wanted a wife. And, obviously, he had selected her to be that wife.

Those were the facts as had been sent to her by a friend in the states who owned a matchmaking business. That friend and her husband had been the ones who first piqued her interest in doing such a strange thing as becoming a mail order bride. Right or wrong, best for her or not, Greta was committed to the experience, and now, to this man named Brigham Whitestar.

It was going to be an interesting escapade quite different from Greta's heritage and current state of living.

Greta was the daughter, the oldest daughter of two, of a Bavarian diplomat who had long encouraged her to find a way to the United States, a new country with lots of promise for young people. Her father had been there, he had seen the prosperity, and what was more, he had followed the westward migration of people who were either gold prospectors or entrepreneurs. Money wasn't an object for her, but the desire to leave her much loved country was. Especially to leave it for parts unknown and a marriage that could be utter disaster.

But the marriage could also be her one chance at happiness - a chance that remaining in Bavaria her whole life might not be realized. She knew the local chaps, and Greta also knew that if one of them wanted to marry her, it would only be for her family's wealth and not for love.

She was an attractive woman, but she was also a little different than most other women in the country of her birth. Greta was highly educated, having a university degree from one of the best colleges in Europe, and she was very choosy about men.

She wanted someone on her level, a man who could talk about national interests, politics and mums. Greta loved mums. She loved all flowers, of course, but mums were her favorite of all.

Moreover, Greta wanted some adventure in her life. The beautiful Bavaria had grown stale in her mind, not the breathtaking scenery or the nature of the hills and valleys, but the everyday life of it. There seemed to be nothing new, nothing to look forward to but more of the same as she had done the previous day.

Having spent four years away from home at the university, Greta knew there was more to life and living than what she had in their mid-sized village and what the country as a whole could give to her.

It was time for a change, so she had written to her friend who had made the journey a couple of years earlier and asked to be listed in the agency's catalogue of women available to men who were searching for a mail order bride.

Greta pulled the long dress from her closet and laid it on her bed. If there aren't dresses available there suitable for a wedding, this one will do, she thought to herself. I can't believe I am going across the ocean to marry someone I've never met. She smiled to herself at the sense of adventure rising in her soul.

From the train leg of her journey, Greta would be on two different luxury ships that would carry her to America by way of other European countries. The journey would be long and hazardous, but she didn't fear the challenge of crossing an ocean in search of a new life.

Three days later, she stood on the small platform of the local train dispatchery with her family behind her waiting for the train that would begin the journey of her lifetime, one which Greta Stein hoped would be the best trip she had ever taken. In her heart, she knew this was a good decision and that only good things would come from it.

When she was settled into her berth, Greta took a seat by the window and waved to her family, not knowing when or if she would ever see them again. Her younger sister had seemed a little traumatized over watching her sister leave home, but Greta had promised she would see her before too much longer, one way or the other.

Tears welled in her eyes while her heart fluttered at the chance of true romance and happiness.

Two months later, both Cody and Brig paced back and forth on the platform of the local train station, anxiously awaiting the arrival of the two women they had selected from the catalogue at Pretty Brides from Back East. It had been a long and suspenseful wait.

Although Brig seemed calmer than Cody on the surface, his heart was beating wildly in anticipation of meeting his bride. The house was clean, the larder was stocked and he had bathed and dressed in his best clothes. First impressions counted, he figured, so he had done his best to put forth his best foot.

Cody, on the other hand, saw the arrival of his woman as just another day like any other day. At least that was the impression he was trying to give, but his body language and constant pacing on the arrival platform bespoke his true emotions. He was excited beyond comprehension. For days, he had imagined a woman in his home, a woman who would soon become his wife. He could see her in his kitchen preparing meals, in his yard tending a garden, in town with him shopping for needed supplies, and most importantly, in his bed making children with him.

Anyone who took notice of the two men might wonder just what had them so polished and anxious. But few, other than the couple at the agency, actually knew that they were meeting their mail order brides today.

A raging thunderstorm was blowing through the town. The ever present wind was even worse, blowing the barrels and ropes hanging on the wall at the station around and about in a frenzy so that both men had to hang onto their hats for dear life.

The sky was a mottled color of puce and frequent lightning washed out the faces of the waiting passengers until they looked like a crowd of ghosts-- all black and white and mostly greys.

They heard the train whistle first, followed by the show of steam from the locomotive puffing up and outwards and spreading into the sky as the metal beast approached.

Brig forced himself to lean against one of the corner posts of the platform and relax the best he could. Certainly he didn't want his bride's first sight of him to be one in which he appeared nervous and overly anxious. That first impression thing again.

But Cody continued to pace back and forth until the stationmaster cut him a strange look, bringing him to a standstill.

"Do you have a photo of your woman?" Cody asked.

Brig shook his head. "The agency said they couldn't get one for me, and they didn't seem overly concerned about looks. As much as told me so, too. I guess it's the woman's character that's most important, after all."

"How will we recognize the two of them?"

"I have a general description of the woman I selected. Thirty-one and from Bavaria, whatever that is supposed to tell me. She is of minor royalty, whatever that means. Highly educated, speaks three languages and quite independent, which is a very good thing out here in the West. That's about all I know."

"Thirty-one? That's old."

"I'm thirty-one. I don't think that's old at all. How old are you?" he asked his obviously younger counterpart.

"Twenty two," Cody answered. "I'm a young whipper snapper."

"You certainly are," Brig answered with the same sarcasm with which Cody had accused him of being "old."

"But, I've lived hard in those short years," Cody retorted, feeling the need to defend his young age. "I'm wise beyond my years."

"Then prove it and quit that nervous pacing," Brig shot back. "You act like a boy who needs to use the potty."

Cody burst out laughing. "I guess you're right," he said, taking a position beside Brig at the post.

"Do you know anything about your woman?" Brig asked Cody.

"Only that she's eighteen and a teacher. And very well proportioned."

Brig smiled to himself. He hadn't given any thought to how his woman would be physically. Actually, he didn't care as long as she had a keen mind and a willingness to help him raise a family and make his cattle businesses prosperous so that those kids would have a good life with deep roots in the valley.

The oncoming train slowed considerably as it approached and the last few yards were at a crawling pace as it came to stop in just the right place, the last shot of steam bellowing out the smokestack and covering those who waited on the platform.

When the ceiling of steam faded away in the wind, both men craned their necks while feigning indifference, but they, along with all the others who waited, were anxious to see who would get off the train.

Excitement permeated the platform with voices rising slightly as the passengers started to stream around the waiting crowd.

As Cody and Brig waiting anxiously, they heard a woman clearing her throat.

They turned around to see a petite woman, dressed conservatively in brown, with one suitcase and one trunk sitting on the old wood of the train station platform. A modest string of pearls lay around her neck and a cameo was pinned to her blouse. She wore her hair upswept into a very tidy bun.

"Are either of you two gentlemen…" she paused and looked at a scribbled note before continuing, "a Mr. Brigham Whitestar?"

Cody's eyes registered an emotion, but it was hard to tell whether it was relief or disappointment. Brig, though, smiled broadly. Cody continued to scan the crowd. Brig removed his hat.

"That's me, ma'am. You must be the lady that the agency sent."

She stuck out her hand toward Brig.

"Yes, I am. Greta Stein. Pleased to meet you…Brigham Whitestar."

"The pleasure is all mine, Miss Stein. Please...call me Brig. My friends do."

"Okay, then Brig it is. Mine call me Greta, and so shall you."

Brig immediately liked the directness she had about her. And she wasn't bad looking either, although very different from the women in the valley who wore their hair down and in ringlets most of the time. He could see the intelligence in her eyes, and he could hear the determination in her voice. Instantly, Brig felt as if he had made the perfect choice for his bride. But, only time would tell.

"I hate to interrupt, but did you see another woman on the train who might have been coming here to meet her husband?" Cody didn't spare any words about the purpose of Greta's trip, and he didn't spare any consideration that she may not want others to know that.

Greta shook her head. "No. Sorry. Was there supposed to be another lady from the agency traveling with me?"

"Yes, there was. Brig and I were at the agency the same day, so we expected the two of you to travel together. Maybe something has happened to her."

"Then perhaps you should be questioning the agency," Greta said, turning back to Brig.

Her offhanded comment seemed just a tad rude, but both Brig and Cody let it slide.

She'll not get along well here with that attitude, Cody thought to himself as he moved a little farther away from the couple. Gradually, he made his way to the agency as Brig and Greta loaded her bags in the carriage Brig had brought to the station. Cody glanced back at them just as he pushed open the door to the agency. He could feel their instant bonding.

"Good morning, Mr. Johnson," the man at the agency said, rising from his chair. "How can I help you this fine morning?"

Cody couldn't believe the man was so exuberant, a fake show of enthusiasm he was sure.

"Well, for starters, my bride wasn't on the train. What is the problem?"

The man's eyes grew wide with surprise. "Well, I don't know, Mr. Johnson. I've not received anything saying she wouldn't be there." He returned to his desk and shuffled around some papers, finally pulling one out from a large stack. He glanced over the paper quickly.

Cody waited impatiently, shifting his weight from one foot to the other.

"Do you mind waiting here for a couple of minutes? I'll run over to the telegraph office and send a wire to her family. Maybe there has been a delay, but they will know."

"I'll check back in a little bit," Cody said, his mouth dry for a beer.

"Sure, that's fine. It should be about an hour at the most before I will know something."

Cody didn't bother to reply. Instead he turned on his heel and left the office for the saloon. It wouldn't be the first time he'd drowned his sorrows in a few beers or shots of whiskey, the automatic answer to a broken man.

In the saloon, the girls were already going at it full steam ahead. As soon as he bellied up to the bar, one of them was by his side.

"Hello there cowboy," she said. "Wanna hunt some cattle with me?"

"No," came Cody's blunt response. "Give me a beer," he said to the bartender without looking at the girl.

"Awww…who licked the red off your candy today?" the girl asked, persistent.

"Nobody licked anything that belonged to me," he answered her without turning.

She laughed. "Well, if you decide that would be of interest to you, just find me. Okay?"

Cody turned to look into one of the cutest faces he had seen in a long time. She was new to the saloon.

"Okay," he said, his voice softer this time. "I'll do that." He watched the girl walk away from him, her narrow waist accenting her perfect behind. Cody's manhood stirred, but his mind held firm.

Two beers later, Cody decided he needed to get home before the temptation of the girl overpowered him. He paid his tab and headed out of the saloon, looking back to find the girl's eyes plastered on him. She puckered up her lips at him in a flirtatious way. He smiled and continued out the swinging doors.

Back at the agency, the man had a telegram in his hand.

"Oh, Mr. Johnson. Seems your bride reconsidered at the last minute. She won't be coming. So, we can do one of two things. Either you can go back through the catalogue or I'll be happy to refund your deposit. Whatever you want to do."

"I'll take a refund," Cody said. "This could go on for a long time, and I don't particularly like my money tied up like that."

"I understand," the man said. He pulled a bag of money from the desk drawer and counted out a stack of bills to Cody. "There you go, sir. I'm sorry it didn't work out. Rare problem, but I guess it is bound to happen sooner than later."

"I guess," Cody said, highly disappointed. He turned to the door and left without any further conversation.

He saw Brig's carriage tied up in front of the coffee shop as he rode out of town.

Back at his house, Cody sat in the kitchen for quite a long time, assessing his emotions about his no-show bride. He didn't exactly feel sorry for himself, but he wasn't happy either. This had been a big let down and a manhood crasher at the same time.

The bouquet of wildflowers he had picked for her that morning sat in a beer stein on the table waiting. Cody Johnson smiled at the flowers as he rose from his chair.

"You're still pretty," he said to the myriad of colors. "Even if she didn't come to see you."

He rode for two hours around his property. The solitude was a peacemaker for a man who had ventured out of his comfort zone only to be stung with embarrassment. It wouldn't happen again.

"This here is my house," Brig told Greta as he opened the door and ushered her into his one bedroom ranch house. Although modest, it was one of the larger homes on the outskirts of the city.

Greta took a quick look round and nodded towards the bedroom. "Please put my things in there and I'll unpack in a little while."

Looking slightly embarrassed, he put her luggage down in one corner by the wardrobe as she watched from the bedroom doorway. Brig felt the need to establish some boundaries immediately.

"Of course you'll sleep here until we're married. I'll take one of the beds out in the bunkhouse."

"That's not necessary," she told him quickly. "Why don't you make up a cot and put it over in the corner of the main room? I know you won't bite."

"Well, thank you for that, and you're right, I don't bite, but I also don't mind sleeping in the bunkhouse. I often do when we have an early morning drive.

She didn't argue with him, so Brig assumed she was only being nice with her offer.

"What time do you get up in the morning?" Greta asked him.

"Well, ma'am, its usually around four. We start early so I can go check on the cows and horses in the barn and feed them."

"Four o'clock?"

"I know that's a little early for most city folks. You've no need to get up then. I'll be quiet and grab a bite to eat later."

She waved her hand in dismissal.

"Nein, Brig. I'll make breakfast for you. After all, we will be married soon and a woman needs to make sure her man has his breakfast before he starts work."

"We'll, thank you. Now, I usually get some burnt eggs, bacon, and beans from the cook over at the bunkhouse. Never was one for making my own food. Never learned how."

"Did you have a housekeeper?"

Brig looked down at the dusty and worn-off leather of his boots.

"I did, but she was an older lady and one day she just...er...got tired of working I guess and I didn't have her anymore. I mean--"

Greta laughed. "I'll make you breakfast tomorrow. German women are known to be good housekeepers."

"I don't want you to be a housekeeper. If you see fit, I want to be your husband and you to be my wife."

"You are a kind man, Brigham Whitestar. Now, let me change into something more suitable and you can show me around your ranch. Yes?"

He sighed with relief. "I'd like that."

He paused for a few moments before continuing.

"Can you ride a horse, Miss Greta? I'm sorry but I don't have any of those fancy ladies' side saddles."

Her smile lit up her face.

"Brigham...I've never used those. I rode horses for my father when he used to race them."

His eyes lit up at this new and useful information.

"Did you win any races?"

"Most often I did. Yes. We had several Arabians that Papa had imported directly from Egypt. I went there with him, helped him to select the ones we wanted and we were with the beautiful animals as the freighter steamed around and into the North Sea. We docked at Hamburg and took the horses down to our home in Bavaria."

Her eyes were happy as she told him this.

"What kind of horses do you race?" Her eyes continued to sparkle with anticipation.

"Quarter horses. Without them, we couldn't have settled the West. They want to please people so much that they'll die first, rather than give up."

"The Arabians are the same way. They are the fastest horses on earth...Brig, but let me try one of your quarter horses. I think that will be fast enough for now."

She shut the door to the bedroom softly so she could change clothes.

Brig whistled as he sat down on his rough couch, looking over to his bedroom where he heard Greta singing softly as she got dressed for their ride. Life was better for him now than it had ever been.

Greta looked amazing sitting atop the handsome quarter horse by the stables while Brig saddled his own. He could tell she was an experienced rider and horse person by the way she held the reins and spoke softly to the steed. Once in his own saddle, he turned to her.

"I don't know which is more handsome, Greta, you or the horse."

"Well, thank you, Brig. This is a fine specimen, I'll have to be first to say it. Did you raise him from a foal?"

"Sure did. Actually, his name is Wing, the son of this horse who we call Eagle. Get the correlation?"

"How fitting," Greta answered dishonestly. She found both names to be quite juvenile and made a mental note to find a way to name the future stock that came from these majestic animals.

"I liked both names. One of my ranch hands named the colt."

Greta sighed with relief that her soon to be husband didn't have anything to do with such a corny name.

"I shall call him Wind on the Wing," she announced with a big dose of authority. "And I might just call him Wind after I see how he performs, that is." She clicked her legs against the young horse's sides and left the stables in an almost blur, Brig watching as the horse stretched out his legs in power.

He kicked Eagle and took out after his woman and her newfound friend.

"Wait for me," he hollered after Greta, but his words were ignored. "Guess she's been cooped up too long," Brig said to himself, knowing that the horse would go to the only place he'd been before; the ridge that overlooked the valley below them.

He took his time, keeping Greta and Wing within his eyesight, loving that she had already displayed her love for horses. I couldn't have picked a more perfect woman for me, Brig thought to himself. What a great match.

Sure enough, as he and Eagle came up the hill to the pinnacle of earth that rose above the valley below, he saw Greta sitting on the large tree trunk left when he and one of the ranch hands had cut down a tree struck by lightening. Wing nibbled the short grass that covered the area just beyond the trunk. Greta was looking out at the valley.

"Have a nice ride?" Brig asked, climbing down from his horse.

"Oh yes," she said, almost dreamily. "I didn't realize how much this two months of travel had affected me. Too much inside and not enough outside, I think."

"It can happen," Brig said, letting go the reins so that Eagle could join Wing with the nibbling.

"So, tell me about yourself, Brig," she said softly.

"What do you want in a wife?"

Brig thought for a couple of minutes before answering, choosing his words carefully.

"Well," he began. "I want a wife who loves the things that I love along with her own things that are separate from that. I want a wife who can make me happy while she is also happy. I want a wife who will help me build this ranch into something that will give our children security and happiness."

"Children?" she asked.

Brig's heart skipped a beat. "Yes, definitely. Don't you want children?" He hoped for only one answer from Greta. Soon, it came.

"Yes. I want many children. You know there are only two in my family, well, my immediate family. I have a sister, but we have lots of cousins. My mother only wanted two children, and she stopped after we were born. A big disappointment to my father, I believe, though he's never said anything."

"We have eight in mine, but I'm the only one out here in Colorado," Brig added. "And I miss the rest of them."

"Why didn't they come, or some of them anyway?"

"Because they are running the family shipping business in Charleston."

"Charleston? Where is that?"

"In South Carolina. Back East. They are all there. My father told me the day I left that I was crazy for coming to Colorado. 'You'll be back in three months,' he said to me."

"And how long have you been here?" Greta was all ears.

"Six years," Brig answered. "Six long and lonely

years."

Silence again. No doubt that Greta was assessing her own situation with a family all the way across the ocean in Bavaria.

"That's a long time. Have you seen them, or any of them?"

"No. Just been me. I've gotten a telegram or two from my mother telling me who has married and who has become engaged. But, so far, none of them have ventured out of Charleston. They are another reason I want to marry. To show them that I can be happy here and can raise a family here."

"I understand," Greta answered him. "That's important to me, too. Although I'm sure that my parents are going to come visit us at some point in time. They are just the type. My father has been to America several times."

"Really?"

"Yes. He's a diplomat, so travel is part of his job. He works in trade negotiations between the European countries and the United States. An envoy, I guess you might call him."

Brig thought about that for a moment, and then cleared his throat.

"The guy at the agency told me you have some royalty in your roots."

Greta laughed aloud. "Well, Brig, sorry, but I don't. Just two loving parents who raised me well, educated me and blessed my decision to come to this new world. Royalty? I don't think so."

They laughed together.

"Darn it!" Brig finally said. "I was sure you'd be unpacking a box of the crown jewels."

"Sorry to disappoint you," she returned.

"Oh, I'm not disappointed at all, trust me."

There was silence for a few moments.

"Speaking of disappointment, who was that young man at the train station today? Do you know him?"

"Not well. He happened to come to the agency office the same day I was there selecting you. Name's Cody Johnson, a young rancher that lives not very far from here, actually. We've never had any business relationship, but I do know who he is."

"Fine looking young man," Greta said in her direct way. "He won't have any problem finding a bride, of that I'm certain."

"Yeah, well, he isn't off to a very good start. She didn't show up here."

"That doesn't mean anything," Greta responded. "Lots of girls think this sort of life sounds romantic and adventuresome, but when it comes time to start packing, things change. They realize it is a forever thing, not just some sort of vacation, so they back out. How old was she? Or do you know?"

"He told me she was eighteen."

"Eighteen? Good heavens, that's just barely legal. He needs someone older, maybe not as old as I am, but certainly older than eighteen. Was he ordering lust or a bride?"

Brig laughed aloud. "I don't know him well enough to answer that, but if I had to guess, I'd say he was ordering a bride out of lust."

They laughed together, but at Cody's expense.

"Seriously," Greta said. "I feel sorry for him. That has to be a disappointment."

"Oh, I'm sure it is," Brig said. "But that has nothing to do with us. I'm happy you came and I'm happy that is you who came. I believe we are going to get along simply fabulous."

Greta turned to him in complete seriousness.

"So do I. Are you ready to ride back to the house? I really need to get unpacked."

"Sure, it's about dinner time anyway." Brig got up from the ground and offered Greta his hand, which she took. He felt a tinge of heat run through his body from his toes to his head, another sign that she was the one.

"I hope you can tolerate one meal from the bunkhouse," Brig said to her on the slow ride back to their house.

"Are you kidding? Don't forget I've been on a train, two boats and another train for the past two months. I'm sure that anything cooked fresh on a stove will taste like heaven to me."

"Good, 'cause I believe the guys have planned a welcome meal for you. This should be interesting."

They rode along slowly with Brig pointing out the different pastures and what kind of cattle were in each of them. The couple had quickly found a point of comfort between them, which Brig hoped would convince her to marry him pretty quickly.

Brig was dreaming about his childhood when the savory odors of cooking bacon drifted to his nose and woke up his brain. He sat upright so quickly that he almost fell off his cot. He inhaled the smell of fresh biscuits and coffee and he knew that a jar of fresh honey would probably be on the table. Greta had said she loved fresh honey.

He pulled on his heavy pants and took his pocket

watch from the small waist pocket. Through still half asleep eyes, Brig strained to tell the time. Finally, the small watch came into focus. It was four o'clock in the morning.

Greta was in the kitchen making breakfast and that made him smile. A beautiful woman, an incredible breakfast, and the whole day in front of him; he hadn't had those types of luxuries for a very long time. Who could ask for more?

He stretched out his arms and made sure he didn't look like the devil. Brig rose from the bed and walked over to the corner of the very large room where Greta was busy cooking.

"Good morning," he said.

"Good morning. You did say four o'clock, didn't you?"

"Yes, I most certainly did. And, I also said that I would grab a bite in the bunkhouse. Actually reminded you of that last night, didn't I?"

"Yes, you most certainly did," she mocked easily. "But, why? I'm perfectly capable of cooking a meal for you and there is no need for you to walk that far to eat breakfast, Brig."

"That's nice of you, and I thank you," he said, sitting down at the table. She made his plate and set it in front of him. Then, she made her own.

The conversation was light as easy as they ate their first meal in their house together. The crew had made a nice celebration dinner of roast and all the trimmings the evening before. Greta had gotten along well with the men, laughing and talking with them. They were charmed by her accent, but even more by having a woman in their midst.

After breakfast, Brig left her alone to unpack and

tidy up the house while he went out to take care of the horses and on to the bunkhouse where the men would begin their day. That part of life wouldn't change just because a new woman had come to join the ranch, but other parts would.

    Brig would always remember his first wife, Mary. Every day he thought of her. Every evening he said a prayer for her soul. She had died when she fell into the well and drowned, a well that he had been remiss about shoring up and covering with a heavy piece of wood. She had told him repeatedly to do that, but other things always seemed to be more important.

    The day of her death was forever plastered in his mind. Brig had been in the far pasture with the men, only five of them then, putting up fence posts in preparation of nailing the railings to them the next day. When he came home for lunch, Brig heard Mary screaming, but he couldn't see her. He finally traced the weakening sounds of her please for help to the spot where the well had been, but it was all caved in.

    He realized that she was buried somewhere beneath that dirt. "Hold on," he had screamed at her as he jumped back on his horse and took off in a gallop towards the pasture to get the men to come help him. When they returned, she was no longer screaming, so he knew she had gone home to be with the Lord that she prayed to every day, several times a day.

    Brig had capped off the well, and eventually, when he got over the first raw anguish of his grief, he dug another well two hundred yards away and made a flower garden over the other one. The flowers grew there every spring and bloomed all summer. He had never replanted the seeds, they came up on their own. Blue ones, all of them, Mary's favorite.

Greta reminded him of Mary a lot.

"There's going to be a horse race in town next month," Brig told Greta that night at dinner. "Interested?"

She thought for a moment before answering. "Do you think Wind is ready for a race?" she asked, buttering her scone.

"I doubt it. What about one of the other horses in the stable. You know there are over twenty out there."

"Yes, but have any of them been trained?" she asked, taking her first bite of the delicious pastry.

"Not for racing particularly, but there are some fast ones."

"Oh, how I wished we had a sturdy Arabian. I'd be on that horse and gone in a flash!" Greta waved her arm to the side as if she were, indeed, a fast horse setting out ahead of the pack.

Brig smiled to himself. He knew where there was a fast Arabian, but he didn't tell Greta.

"Well, my dear, we don't have one. Yet."

She smiled, her second nature telling her that Brig would eventually get her an Arabian, and she promised herself that she would race it the next time a race was held on Community Day in the valley.

"Have you given any thought as to when we should get married?" he finally asked, the question looming in his mind for the past several days. She had been there for two weeks already, and nothing had been said about marriage. Brig was getting tired of sleeping on the horsehair cot. It was time to be back in his feather bed.

"Not really. What do you think?"

"I think its time," Brig answered. "How is next week? I can make all the arrangements when we go into town for the horse race tomorrow."

"Sure," Greta answered, as if he were only asking about what color fabric she wanted.

"Do you have a dress? Everything you need?"

"I do," she said. "Brought it with me."

How could he have doubted that she would be fully prepared already? Greta was the epitome of efficiency with everything, from cooking to gardening to marriage. He smiled to himself. Now, he knew the perfect opportunity to give her a horse that she really wanted.

The next week, in a quiet little ceremony with only Greta, Brig and two of the ranch hands, they were married. As they were leaving the Justice of the Peace's office, Cody Johnson stepped out of the saloon just as Brig and Greta were walking to the small coffee shop.

"Well, hello," Cody slurred. "How's the married couple?"

Brig knew instantly that Cody was sloshed. He stepped around Greta to be between Cody and his new wife.

"We're just fine. I see you're not feeling any pain either." Brig could have kicked himself at the blunder. It sounded as if he were picking a fight - or argument - with Cody.

"Nope. Try not to," Cody said, and ambled on off down the wooden sidewalk that connected the stores.

"That wasn't necessary," Greta said. "Leave him to his disappointment, Brig. You don't have to drive the point home."

Brig was instantly sorry and thought about going to apologize to Cody.

"Wait here," he told Greta. "I'll be right back." But as he turned to go to Cody, the younger man and his horse came flying by at a breakneck speed, heading out of town. He had missed the opportunity.

"Don't do that again," Greta warned. "You never know when will be the last time you speak to someone. Always try to make it a good and memorable event."

They ate a sandwich for their first lunch as man and wife. But it was a very quiet lunch as Brig's mind went right back to that well.

When they got home, Greta went into the house and Brig went to the stables to see if the horse had been brought over. It had. And a fine looking mare she was. Young, with a wedge-shaped head sporting a broad forehead. Her eyes were large, her muzzle was small and her nostrils looked as if they had been drawn into her face, large as they were.

She was soot black, and her tail sat high on her haunches. Brig knew she was a champion and that she would make Greta a fine, fine horse. He led her by the bridle into the training circle by the stables.

"Greta!" he called into the house from the back door. "Come here."

Brig heard the material of her gown swishing as she walked through the house to the door.

"What?"

"Come here, I have something to show you." He opened the door and helped Greta out of the house. Holding her hand they crossed the yard toward the stables.

"Close your eyes."

She did and he led her about twenty yards around the edge of the stables.

"Okay. Open them."

Brig watched as the smile slowly formed on her mouth and her eyes began to sparkle.

"Lady," she said underneath her breath, climbing onto the lowest rung of the fence with her tiny feet. "Come here, Lady."

Brig was confused. "Who is Lady?"

"My first horse," Greta said. "She looked just like this."

Hours later, the two of them climbed into bed together for the first time. They consummated the marriage with great tenderness for each other, and then they fell asleep in each other's arms; Brig dreaming about children and Greta dreaming about Lady. Theirs was a wonderful world.

The town square had been decorated for the parade, band performance, and after that, the start of the horse race, which looped around town once then headed off into the surrounding countryside before circling back into town.

Greta was racing the Arabian mare Desert Lady and Cody was on his black stallion, Abyss. Cody, Brig and Greta had run into each other occasionally but the interaction was always terse, with Cody seemingly angrier each time they saw him - if he was sober, which was often.

Brig knew it was because he didn't get his mail order bride and he felt sorry for the other man, especially since his own match was turning out so well. Greta made the meals for the two of them, and she reveled in the ownership of Lady, taking care of her personally, even though there were ranch hands to do it for her.

Cody, on the other hand, was becoming more frustrated every day. He'd always been jealous of Brig, the more affluent rancher who, in Cody's own opinion, had a far better life than he'd had. Getting a mail order bride didn't always end in a marriage but it usually did and now, Brig had proven his choice of women had been a good one. Still, he felt sorry for Cody Johnson.

A large crowd had gathered for the horse race, and they were very surprised that a woman was jockeying a horse, and especially one as spirited as Brig's Arabian. What they didn't know was that Greta was an experienced horsewoman by her own credentials, all of which she had brought to America with her.

Brig had nothing to do with it.

The women were aghast that she was even riding, much less in a black outfit of pants and top hat, which she threw over to Brig as the time to begin drew closer. Greta pinned her long hair up quickly and climbed into the saddle that waited for her on Lady's back.

The men held the horses steady as the riders mounted their respective animals. Cody almost took off too early due to his spirited horse that could smell competition, but all the riders managed to stay behind the starting line until someone dropped a flag and they were off.

Brig tried to discourage Greta about the pants, but she only flicked off his warning, saying that she'd worn them in Germany when she was a girl so she didn't see any difference riding them for a horse race in the middle of nowhere. He couldn't argue with her, because after all, the pants were eminently practical.

Both Cody and Greta were quickly out front as the horses jumped off the starting line. Each of them jockeyed for the lead position as they raced along the street through town and out into the countryside. Brig mounted his own horse to follow behind the ten or so racers who had just passed by him. He needed to keep a check on his wife.

Greta never broke a sweat as she looked across at the young man racing beside her and the rivulets of sweat running down his face. She nodded at him.

Cody nodded back and urged his black horse even faster, but he couldn't quite get ahead of her until Greta pulled back her reins slightly and let him. Then, she kicked her horse hard and passed Cody again, smiling at him as she passed by with little effort.

Not to be outdone, Cody popped the whip at his horse, sped up and passed Greta. They raced like this, first one and then the other in the lead. The rest of the pack was behind them, the closest being several yards back. It was a neck and neck race all the way back to town.

As they came barreling into the narrow path the crowd had left, Greta and Cody were nose to nose, and remained such until they crossed the finish line. As they brought their steeds to a slow walk and turned back to saunter to the grandstand, she smiled at Cody.

"Great race," she said to him.

"Where the hell did you learn to ride like that?" he asked her.

"Bavaria," she said quietly. "In Germany."

"I know where Bavaria is," Cody answered in a not so friendly manner.

"Okay, I was just making sure," Greta said. "I never know around here." She climbed off her horse and looked through the crowd for Brig, but she didn't seem him anywhere. Then, a finger tapped on her shoulder. She turned to face her husband, his mouth puckered for a kiss.

She kissed him and turned back to Cody.

"Good race," she said, and led her horse away.

After much conferring at the judges' stand, Greta was declared the winner of the race. Half the crowd mumbled, the other half cheered, but Greta stepped to the podium and a hush fell.

What did she expect? A prize?

"Ah," the announcer said. "Miss, ah, what is your name again?"

She didn't let the insult go unnoticed.

"The same name as is on that registration form," Greta replied, her eyes meeting the man's with steely emotions. "Can you read?"

The crowd burst out laughing at her zinger. It was just that fast that Greta became the most popular lady in town. Brig grinned with pride that his wife, an independent and strong-headed woman had just one-upped the mayor without even knowing it.

"So, what's my prize?" she asked, relishing in the attention.

"Ah, ma'am," the mayor said. "We don't have a

prize. You just win and that's it." He didn't want to tell her that normally, the winner got rounds and rounds of drinks at the saloon.

"Then we'll have to change that," Greta said, stepping down from the podium. Brig was there to help her.

"Good show," he said, kissing her cheek.

"We have to find some prizes before the next race," she said. "Let's find Cody."

They found him at the bar in the saloon. Greta accepted the congratulations of people as she and Brig walked over to join him.

"Nice race," she said to the man she had just beaten. "That stallion of yours has some real muscle."

"And so does your Arabian," he said. He offered her his hand.

She took it, shook it, and kept holding it.

"I know you're disappointed about a bride," she began. "But I know someone who would be a perfect match for you."

"Who is it?"

"I don't want to say until I contact her myself. If she's interested, I will tell you then. Is that okay?"

Cody shrugged his shoulders. "I guess it will have to be, not a lot of choice. Is she coming through that same agency? If so, I'm not interested."

"No, not through the agency. I know this person myself. I'll send a telegram if you like."

"I would like," Cody said. "I would definitely like." He figured that if Greta knew her, the woman would most likely be as spirited as Brig's wife. Just the kind of woman he needed. And wanted.

"Then I'll do it," Greta said. She took Brig's hand. "Let's go to the telegraph office and I'll send a wire immediately." They began to walk away.

"How old is she?" Cody called out to Greta.

Greta turned around to face him. "She's older than eighteen," she answered, not intending to be rude or short with her new friend.

Before she and Brig could get out the door of the saloon, the crowd parted and the mayor was standing there, facing Greta.

"It was terrible that there wasn't a prize for winning that race," he said. "So this has been donated for you." He held out a bouquet of roses and a saddle.

Brig quickly stepped forward and took the items from the mayor.

"Well, how nice!" Greta said. "Please thank whoever donated them for me. I love that saddle and the flowers are beautiful!"

They went outside the saloon where the men had taken all the horses that had raced and tied them under the shade trees to cool off and get water. Greta checked on Lady to make sure she was okay and then went on to the boarding house where she and Brig had rented a room for the afternoon so she could change clothes.

"You are a star, my love," Brig said, pulling her into his arms.

"Thank you," Greta said, pecking him on the cheek.

"That's not a kiss a wife gives her husband," he said, positioning his mouth over hers in a long and lingering kiss. Finally she pushed him away.

"Save that for tonight," she said. "We need to get that telegram sent as soon as possible so that if she's interested, plans can be made."

"Were you serious about that?" Brig didn't doubt her, but he didn't put much thought into whether she was serious or not at the moment Greta had told Cody about someone she knew.

"Of course I was serious." She quickly pulled off her pants and riding coat and slid effortlessly into her day dress. Brig watched as she made no move toward modesty.

"I simply love you, Greta Whitestar."

"I love you, too, Brigham Whitestar."

Greta changed into a cool cotton dress and brushed her hair, pulling it back with large jeweled pins. They went back out into the street and the crowd. She linked hands with Brig, they strolled through the picnic and children's area and ate some cherry pie and ice cream. She got some pie juice on her chin, and Brig lovingly wiped it off for her while she laughed.

They went to the telegraph office where Brig talked with men outside on the wooden sidewalk while Greta sent her telegram. She came over to join him when she was through.

"All done?" he asked her.

"Yes, thank you."

Brig saw Cody across the street wiping the sweat and dust off his face. Cody glared over at them sullenly, and then wandered off somewhere. Brig found him a half hour later drinking whiskey at a bar, which had been set up on the edge of the street. By the looks of it, many men were getting drunker by the minute.

He took Greta over to a picnic bench in the shade after they'd gotten hot in the sun and they chatted for a while.

He ran a finger around the inside of his shirt collar then looked up as a drunk Cody wandered over. He looked directly at Greta and ignored Brig.

"You know, if you find yourself bored with the old man here, I'll come rescue you."

Greta looked shocked and Brig stood up, indignant.

"That's disrespectful, Cody. Leave off and go do something else." Brig did not want any trouble with Cody.

Cody pushed Brig on the chest with his finger and the older man fell back a few steps because it was unexpected.

"Take your hands off me, Cody."

"No," he told him and pushed him again, so Brig clenched his fist and punched him.

Cody slipped and fell down, unable to balance himself with the alcohol flowing through his veins. He staggered to his feet and the fight started.

After a moment or two, several bigger men held them off each other, stopping the fight. Greta had screamed at Brig to not hit Cody anymore.

"He's drunk!" she screamed at her husband. "Just let's go home." Greta gathered up her cotton purse and headed for the boarding house, determined not to have anything else to do with her husband and the fight.

Brig felt his jaw and looked around for Greta, but she was nowhere to be seen. Finally, he asked a woman standing close by.

"Did you see my wife go somewhere, Mrs. Young?"

"She went towards the boarding house, crying."

Brig glared at the still struggling Cody.

"If you've hurt her in any way, there'll be hell to pay. Just leave us alone."

He walked over to the boarding house to find his wife. Steam was coming from his ears, he was so mad. At Cody, but a little perturbed with Greta, too. She had defended Cody.

Brig went straight to the room they had gotten for the afternoon. He knocked on the door.

"Greta?" he called softly.

No answer.

"Greta, honey. Open the door." It was locked from the inside and he was too embarrassed to go to the desk for another key.

Still nothing, but he was certain his wife was in the room. Visibly shaken, he went downstairs and waited for her in the parlor of the boarding house. He had his hat in his hands, twirling the brim around over and over again as he waited for her.

It had been fifteen minutes and he was worried.

What if she's sorry she's married me already? Maybe she thinks I'm a lout and disrespectful and all I want is to be with a woman...well, in a way that a woman like Greta has to think about first before she even considers it. Then he thought, I'm getting way ahead of myself here. First, I have to find out how she's feeling about this whole mess.

Mrs. Smith, a lady of indeterminable age who ran the boarding house and who'd been in town for as long as Brig had, told him that Greta had paid for a month ahead, saying it would be all the time she needed.

Brig looked up when he heard a woman's boot step on the top of the staircase.

It was her.

She came over to him immediately and sat down on the sofa close to him.

"I...I'm sorry for causing all that ruckus. You know men...sometimes they let their emotions get away from them."

Brig took a very deep breath, held her hand carefully, and looked directly into her eyes, pleadingly. He was swept off his feet by her already, and if he had offended her, he was full of remorse for having done so.

She withdrew her hand and held it up. "Before you say anything I also have something to tell you." She paused. "I've been really thinking about Cody. He's a nice man who has a broken heart, Brig, and he's jealous of you, of us. Don't you see that?"

Brig slowly shook his head yes. "I understand."

"And the person I've just telegraphed to see if she'd be interested in coming to America is my sister."

Brig's eyes grew wide with surprise. "Your sister?"

"Yes. The last thing she said to me was to remember her if I found a suitable bachelor. And, I think he is the perfect match for her."

Brig had to think about that for several minutes. If Cody married Greta's sister, the two men would be brother in laws - married to sisters. That wouldn't be so bad, really, and it would ensure that Greta planned to stay with him. That was a huge relief.

"Gosh!" is all that Brig could say until he caught his breath. Then, he squeezed Greta's hand.

"What a perfect answer for Cody," he finally said. "Want to go have some dinner before we go back home?"

"That would be perfect," Greta answered. "I'm

starving."

When they went outside, Cody was gone and the band had begun to play. Greta and Brig ate at the same little coffee shop where they had lunched twice before.

Their ride home was quiet and peaceful; a vast difference from the folly that took place in their bedroom that night. Life was now very, very good.

Sofia read the telegram again, her heart beating rapidly. She clenched the thin paper to her chest and raised her eyes to the heavens. Her prayers had been answered. She ran down the stairs to find her mother, the telegram dangling from her hand.

"Mother, Mother!" she shouted as she ran through the downstairs hallway.

Mrs. Stein stepped out of the library. "I'm here," she said, wondering what in the world had her youngest daughter in such a tizzy.

Sofia came running up to her waving the telegram. "I've gotten a telegram from Greta!"

Mrs. Stein raised her reading glasses to her eyes as she took the telegram from Sofia. "Let me see it." She quietly read the words on the paper, not letting her emotions show themselves.

"I see," she said, a tinge of sternness in her voice.

"Mother! That is wonderful! What she says in there. She's found a husband for me and I can go to America and get married and I'll be with Greta and…"

"Shush!" Mrs. Stein said. "Your father isn't even

here, Sofia. You cannot go without his blessing. You know that, and he won't be back for another month."

"Oh Mother, please don't make me wait. Send Father a telegram, tell him about this. I'm sure he would love for me to go."

"I'm not so sure," Mrs. Stein said, laying the telegram on the hall table. "Let me gather myself and we'll go send him a telegram and ask. But, you know there are no promises, Sofia, so don't get your hopes up."

"I won't," the younger girl said. "But, I'm twenty one now, so there isn't a lot that he can do to stop me."

Mrs. Stein turned back to her daughter. "Don't go making threats, young lady. That is one sure way to keep yourself in Bavaria."

Sofia knew that to be the truth, so she waited on the hall divan until her mother was ready to go to the telegraph office. But in her heart, she knew her father would put his stamp of approval on the move. He always did what his daughters wanted.

Two days later, Mrs. Stein called her daughter downstairs. When Sofia came into the study, her mother had a look of sadness on her face.

"What's wrong, Mother?"

Mrs. Stein pushed the telegram over to her daughter. "You read it."

Sofia picked up the thin paper and scanned it. "Oh my," she said. "He wants you and me to come to America, Mother! Both of us…this is the best day of my life!" She whirled around and around in the library.

"Settle down, Sofia," her mother said. "We have to start packing immediately. We're leaving tomorrow. Your father has already bought the tickets for us. And, he's telegraphed Greta that we're coming - all of us. Father is joining us in Charleston, South Carolina to make the trip to Colorado. It's going to be a family reunion."

It was a whirlwind of activity around the Stein household as both women made ready for a two-month trip to the New World…and hopefully, a brand new life.

Both Brig and Greta rode into town to find Cody and give him the news. They didn't plan to tell him that it was Sofia who was coming to marry him as that might not set well with Cody. He and Brig had been barely on speaking terms after the skirmish after the horse race months before. Distance was safer than chance fighting.

As usual, they found him at the saloon, but he was stone sober. Had been since the day of the Community Celebration. Brig went in and brought him outside to their carriage.

"Greta has something to tell you," Brig had said to Cody. "She's outside in the carriage." He turned and walked back out of the saloon, not sure if Cody would follow him or not. He did.

At the carriage, Greta was smiling broadly. "I've gotten an answer to my telegram," she said.

"And?" Cody wanted to be excited, but he couldn't brace himself for another heartbreak of disappointment. Deep inside himself, though, he knew the woman must have accepted or Greta wouldn't have come to tell him in person.

"She's accepted, Cody."

In his mind, the lights seemed to all come on at once.

"She'll be here in about two months, maybe even less since they are coming a different route."

"They?" Cody and Brig asked at the same time.

"Yes, they. My parents are coming with her to make sure she gets here safely and to see me, meet Brig, and stay with us for a month."

Cody whooped and hollered, jumping up and down. People passing by on the street and the sidewalk thought he was drunk again, but he wasn't. Well, not with liquor, but with happiness. In an instant, his life had begun to turn around.

Two months later, with Greta's stomach showing her pregnancy and Brig looking all proud and spiffed up, they stood at the train station on the exact spot where Greta had arrived a year earlier.

"Do you think he'll ever stop pacing?" Greta asked her husband, as they studied Cody at the end of the platform, squinting out along the tracks as if waiting for his destiny to arrive from across the desert.

"Nope. Not until the train arrives." He laughed.

"Well, at least this time we know she'll be on there. I can't wait to see his face when he finds out it is my sister that is coming to marry him."

They watched as Cody paced in front of them again.

"Do you think that will make a difference?" Greta asked her husband.

"It could only be a plus that Sofia is your sister, my dear. What man wouldn't want a woman like you? The answer is 'no man.'"

Greta thought for several moments. "She's actually very sweet and just the right age for him. I knew the moment I met Cody that they were meant for each other."

"Well I'll be! Not only can she cook, make love, and ride horses in races with men, but she's a matchmaker, too, my wife." Brig took her hand in his. "I'm kidding, of course. I am so damn proud of you, Greta, and the way you've just fit right into my life and this town."

She leaned over and kissed his cheek. "You've made me proud, too, Mr. Mayor."

It was true. Just the week before, the townspeople had elected him mayor, satisfying one of Brig's goals, to be come governor of Colorado one day. But that was in the very distant future; he had things to do at home for now. Maybe in another ten years when their youngest would be about five, that timing would be perfect. Brig squeezed Greta's hand and started to say something.

But, the train whistle cut him off as the locomotive rounded the bend and Cody craned his neck so much that Brig yelled at him.

"Step back or you'll be hit, Cody!"

Cody jumped back, flashed Brig a smile, and then waited another couple of minutes for the train to pull in and come to a complete stop.

All three of them kept looking at the passenger car, their eyes plastered to the steps where people got off. After a short while a young woman carrying a small suitcase in her hand appeared at the top of the steps.

"Sofia! Sofia!" Greta screamed, leaving Brig and Cody standing in their spots while she made her way through the crowd to her sister. The two women met on the platform and wrapped each other tightly in a long hug. Brig and Cody waited patiently, giving them time to reunite.

Next came her parents. Greta was overcome with joy, tears streamed from her eyes. It was in that instant that Brig fully realized what his wife had given up to come join him in a strange land.

The two men waited for the family to be reunited and get through their greeting. Then slowly, they move toward Brig and Cody as if no other person existed on the station platform.

Brig watched his father and mother in law walk slowly through the crowd, still talking with Greta. The man was very distinguished, his top hat in his hand and his arm around the small waist of his very attractive wife. People stared at them, sensing how important the man and woman must be.

Finally they came alongside Brig and Cody.

"Cody," Greta began. "Please meet Sofia, the woman I've been telling you about. She's come from Bavaria just like me."

Cody Johnson blushed as he looked into the blue eyes of the most beautiful girl he had ever seen.

"Pleased to meet you," he said, wiping his hands on his jeans before offering it to her.

Sofia was mesmerized by his handsomeness and his ruggedness. She felt absolutely faint with dizziness at the looks of this man who would become her husband.

"So am I," she managed to say. "So am I."

Cody realized instantly why the two women were friends. Not only did they look alike, but Sofia was bold just as Greta had always been.

"And Brig," Greta went right along. "These are my parents, Mr. and Mrs. Stein. Mom and Dad, this is my husband, Brig."

The three of them shook hands while Cody and Sofia stared into each other's eyes.

"Sofia?" Greta said. "Please, meet my husband, Brig."

Sofia turned to Brig and offered her hand in greeting. "Nice to meet you, Brig. I've learned so much about you from Greta's letters."

"Well, I hope you aren't disappointed," he said, smiling broadly at the pretty young woman. "Welcome to Marlboro Valley."

"Thank you. I am very pleasantly surprised at the beauty of the land here," Sofia said, trying to be sophisticated.

"Brig is the mayor of our fine town," Greta continued. "I'm so very proud of him."

That struck up a chord of compatibility between Brig and Mr. Stein, who took Brig by the arm and led him to the steps down the platform. Following behind them were Greta and her mother, and bringing up the rear were Cody and Sophia.

The four of them languished at the café over sandwiches and coffee while Cody and Sophia sat at another table getting to know each other. By the sound of the young people's laughter and such, it was easy to tell what a perfect matchmaker Greta had been.

As the evening came upon them, Brig took Greta aside.

"Do you think those two will make it until morning?" he asked his wife. "I mean they are already holding hands."

"Do they have to?" Greta asked. "I mean, Brig, it took us weeks, but this is different. I'll ask my parents."

Back at the table, they four older members of the family discussed it. Finally, Mr. Stein went over to Cody and Sophia's table where he talked for a few minutes. He returned to his wife's side with a smile on his face.

"Are you in a hurry to get to Brig and Greta's house?"

"Not particularly," she answered. "Why?"

"Because, and this is if it is okay with the mayor and his wife, you daughter wants to get married."

"Now?" Mrs. Stein asked.

"Now," her husband answered.

The four of them gathered around the young couple as they took each other's hands.

"Cody Johnson, do you take this woman to be your lawful wedded wife?"

And the rest will soon be history.

THE END

Doreen Milstead

Mail Order Bride: From France To The Other Side Of Paradise

Synopsis: Mail Order Bride: From France To The Other Side Of Paradise - A Frenchwoman makes a long and arduous journey to a small town in California. When she arrives, her journey is not complete and the trek to her future husband is as dangerous as the much longer one across the ocean and across America. Her fiancé is a mysterious man but it's the ultimate surprise, which he springs on her that shakes her to the core.

   Marianne sat on her case and watched the rain pour off the veranda and turn the street into red-colored mud. She stood and walked the wooden slats as far as the roof would protect her. Beneath her feet the water ran in rivulets, picking up the dirt of the town, carrying it, spinning back down towards the creek.
   Marianne pushed the wire door stepped into the office. The postmistress, still seated behind the counter, spoke without looking up. "Don't look much

like paradise today, does it, dear?"

"No," said Marianne. "Not much like paradise." She considered the bundles all piled up in one corner, some of which were hers. She ran her hand along the polished oak counter and dinged the bell to see if it would work.

The postmistress frowned. "Springtime comes like this in these parts. The mountains have their way with the weather. And there's not much you or I, or anyone else can do about it. Best just take a seat and wait."

"How long?"

"Until the postmaster returns and the rain abates."

Marianne put her elbows on the counter. The postmistress took a handkerchief and dabbed away a few blobs of mud that had splashed up onto the girl's face, staining her cheek like tears.

"Just an instinct, I believe," she said, on seeing Marianne jut out her chin in indignation. "On account of my own daughters always having dirty faces. Never could stand to look at it." She smiled at Marianne. "Now, I think I'll be drinking some tea."

"Coffee, please" said Marianne and went back out to the porch.

The postmistress brought tin mugs and they drank outside, the steam rising in the wet air. Marianne sat on her case as she had become used to doing. The coffee was bitter and grainy and it seemed to Marianne to be much like the mud that swirled beneath her. But it was warm and she drank it nevertheless.

"You must be tired," said the postmistress.
Marianne nodded.

"Its not a good journey for young lady to do on her own. A whole five days on the steamer."

"I was with the post," said Marianne. "There was always someone. I believe I was quite safe."

"I believe you might say that this office is a civilizing influence. Ten years before, all we saw in these parts was prospectors and fur-trappers. That sort would rob you as quick as look at you"

"But still," said the postmistress, "a long journey." She sipped her coffee. "A long journey." Then like a sacred text, she recited. "Sacramento, Olive Heights, Linda, Sidds Landing, Bright Falls, Monks Crossing, Santa Cruz, Tukesville, Bents Hole, Black Lake, St Marks, Gridley, Araville, Magnolia and Paradise."

"Yes," said Marianne. "And now Paradise."

"And before Sacramento?" asked the postmistress. "

"The East."

"The East?"

Marianne nodded. She remembered. Sacramento, Carston, Donner Pass, Sierra, Bear River, Comstode Lode, the Truckee River, and all the endless other places, some not much more than signs by the railroad, back over the mountains and over the plains, back to the cities and factories and smoke of the East, back to the gray of the sea. All running back to the day she had stepped out of her home and did not look back. All those places were dots on a map she had joined on journey her to here. On this porch, with the rain and the postmistress standing beside her.

"Now, I do believe this is my husband," the postmistress said. A figure on horseback battled through the curtain of rain. His wide-brimmed hat and cape hung heavy, but he rode briskly, his back bolt upright. He paused at the corner of the post office and looked down on Marianne as if seeing an aberration; he glanced at his wife before jerking the rein and taking the horse to the stables.

"Well, now," said the postmistress. "He will see to the horses and when he dries himself down, we will see you organized." She smiled and went inside.

Marianne heard him in the room. He was moving the parcels, angrily stacking them against the wall, as if the persistence of the rain infuriated him. He spoke to his wife, spraying her with questions. Then the door swung open and he stepped onto the porch.

His curly hair was dark. He had a beard and mustache and walked with a limp. Marianne stood. His dark eyes were small and they examined her quizzically. He looked at her case and the bundles beside her.

"This," he said, turning to his wife. "This," he repeated. "This is the order?" He looked at each of them in turn, as if they had tried to play on him a poor quality joke. "This is the parcel for Jackson Ranch?"

He didn't wait for an answer, stepping back inside and emerging again a few moments later with an envelope of documents tied together with string. He untied them, took a set of pince-nez from his top pocket and balanced them on his nose. He frowned. They waited.

He signaled his wife to hand him Marianne's documents and he scrutinized them too. Finally, he bent one knee to examine the label on Marianne's case. He straightened himself, holding on to the wall for balance, as if the leg would not work quite well on its own.

"So," he said, gazing over the frame of his pince-nez, "you are the item listed here as Le Tonnelier Suzette Marianne?"

"Yes, I am Marianne."

"Quite," he nodded. "And you have come from," he consulted the sheaf of documents again. "Merville."

"Yes."

"Merville, Louisiana?"

Marianne shook her head. "From France."

"Ah," said the postmaster. "From France. I see." He returned his pince-nez to his top pocket and carefully put away the documents. "Well," he said. "That coffee does smell good."

Marianne shrugged. "It is warm."

"Warm would suit me just fine right now. I am chilled to the bone. Sarah, I'm hoping here's more in the pot?"

His wife nodded. "Excellent. More coffee for you Miss Marianne," he said and took the mug from her hand.

A horse and cart moved slowly up the street barely visibly through the rain. Marianne heard her name spoken through the wall. Though the rain drummed on the roof and the postmaster's voice distorted she heard Sarah say something about her skin being as white as fine-bone china.

"Well, now Marianne," said the postmaster when he returned. "It was very rude of me not to introduce myself. Especially as now we know who you are," he said, handing her the coffee. "I am Mackenzie and I am the postmaster here in Paradise. And this lady who you know by now is Sarah, my wife."

"And what now?" asked Marianne.

"Of course," said Mackenzie. "You must complete your journey. Your documents are in good order. You are to be delivered to Mr. William Jackson, Jackson Ranch, Paradise. It has all been paid for."

"So," said Marianne, putting down her coffee. "There is no need for delay. If you could direct me to the Jackson home, I might leave."

"No, I cannot do that," said Mackenzie.

"You cannot. What is this? You must."

"I mean I must ensure that you are delivered there. That is what has been paid for. And I will take you there myself, but only after the rain has cleared."

"The rain," said Marianne. "I cannot sit here waiting for the weather. If you decide not to help me with my possessions, you need not worry, because I shall take them myself. But tell me where in Paradise I should go."

"It is not possible," said Mackenzie. "Jackson Ranch is not in Paradise."

"Not Paradise," said Marianne. "But it is. The address. It is written."

"It is," said Mackenzie. "Jackson Ranch, Paradise, California. And that is correct. But the ranch is not in the town of Paradise. It is at the head of the valley, a good half-day's ride from here. And its not a journey you or I, or anyone will make before the weather changes."

"Not in Paradise," said Marianne.

"No," said Mackenzie. "Not exactly. But the truth is its closer to Paradise than anywhere else."

And so they waited and the rain continued to fall for another hour until splashed up beneath the slats and ran in great streams down the center of the town. Towards noon it slowed and the drumming on the roof quieted. Rain fell for a while in intermittent squalls and then it was over. Almost immediately, the clouds broke and sunlight angled down on the valley, fiercely as if trying to make up for lost time.

Mackenzie stood on the veranda and watched the clouds lift out of the valley. He said, "We will eat lunch, I will ready the horse and dougherty, you, Miss Marianne, will ready yourself, and we shall head out. You will eat with us, of course."

They ate a meal of dumplings and gravy on the table in the kitchen at the back of the building. They ate in silence until Mackenzie scraped the gravy from his plate, took a long drink of water and thanked his wife for a wonderful meal. He stood and took his plates to the washbasin.

"I won't condone it," said Sarah, suddenly.

Mackenzie took her plates also and ladled the remaining gravy onto Marianne's plate.

"Do you hear me?" said Sarah.

"It makes no difference," said Mackenzie. "It makes no difference what we think."

"Of course, it makes a difference. It is you who is carrying it out."

"It is me on behalf of this office. I am doing my job."

"Your job," Sarah laughed. "Since when has this been your job?"

"We are responsible for delivering the post."

"She is not the post, she is a child."

"I am not a child," protested Marianne.

"Be quiet," said Sarah.

Mackenzie had been staring out the small window

towards the yard and the stable. Now he turned to face his wife. "The documents are in order, the bill has been paid in full. There is no possible reason not to complete the delivery."

"Perhaps her," said Sarah pointing to Marianne who was wiping the last of the gravy with a dumpling. "Would it be too much to ask you to consider her, for one moment?"

"What is there to consider? She wants to go, it is clear. If she didn't want to go, I would not make her. Of course, I would not." He took the plate away from Marianne and dropped it in the basin. "If she didn't want to go, she wouldn't even be here. She's crossed half the globe and you want me to stop her here, hours from her destination"

Sarah turned to Marianne. "Do you want to go up to Jackson Ranch?"

Marianne held her glass in her hand. She looked at both of them in turn. "But, yes. Of course."

"Are you sure?" asked Mackenzie.

"Certainly."

"There," he said and turned back to scrubbing the plates.

"Why?" asked Sarah.

"Pardon."

"Why do you want to go up to Jackson Ranch?"

Marianne looked confused. "Why," she said. "Because . . ."

"Yes?"

"Because I am to marry."

"You are going marry William Jackson?"

"Yes," said Marianne. "It is arranged."

"I see," said Sarah. "This is all arranged in advance."

"It is. We wrote many letters. I understand everything." Marianne rose from the table. "Now I must ready myself."

"Wait," said Sarah. "Which William Jackson?"

"What do you mean?"

"Which William Jackson are you to marry? William Jackson Junior or William Jackson Senior?"

Marianne hesitated. "I don't understand."

"Young William Jackson or old William Jackson?"

"I think, old."

"And what do you know of him, old William Jackson, your husband to be?"

"I know he is rich. I know he is kind and writes beautiful letters. I know that he is handsome."

Sarah laughed. "You know this. You know this from France. Well you know more of William Jackson and Jackson Ranch than we do in Paradise. And do you know he had a wife?"

Marianne nodded. "He told me."

"And that she is no more?"

"Yes."

"This is wrong," Sarah said, quietly. She turned to her husband. "I know your views are in accordance with mine."

"How old are you?" asked Mackenzie.

"Twenty-five."

"She's lying."

"I do not lie. I will be twenty-five in April. We plan to marry in May. It was a condition. He insisted. He would not marry until I was twenty-five."

Mackenzie shrugged. "There is nothing wrong here. Indeed, I'm surprised you should find fault with a woman marrying into greater experience."

Sarah rose from the table. "I want no part of

this," she said.

Mackenzie prepared the dougherty, harnessed the horse and brought them round to the front of the post office. The sun shone down on the street and the puddles were steaming. Marianne waited on the porch with her belongings packed in a case and several bundled parcels.

"You'll have to wait," said Mackenzie. "Its not just you and your things Jackson is having delivered."

He brought out several bundles from the office, checked them against a list and packed them tightly at the front of the dougherty. He turned to Marianne. "There will be just enough room for you and your cases now."

Marianne looked over his shoulder across the street. A man ambled towards them. He was small and bow-legged and he looked peculiar as he danced around deep ruts filled with water.

"Bill," said Mackenzie. "How may I help you?"

Bill spat black tobacco juice, before touching the brim of his hat. "Mackenzie," he said, "good day to you." He turned to Marianne and gazed for a moment too long. "Miss," he said. Bill nodded at the dougherty. "I gets the impression you are hauling up to Jackson now the weather's cleared."

"That's right," said Mackenzie. "Be all I can do to get back before night falls too."

"Was a terrible storm and that's the truth." Bill smiled at Marianne.

"It was," said Mackenzie. "Now, if you'd excuse us."

"Jackson fair-warned me you might be going up there today. You see he's got a month's supplies ready to take up. Now, I wondered, as you are going up there anyway..."

"I can't, Bill. You know that. I take the post and the post only."

"Sure, that's clear. We all know that. But it seems kind of crazy me going up there at the same time you do. Sure would be helping me out here, Mackenzie."

Mackenzie shook his head, but he didn't seem sure.

"And it would free up some time for me trying to get those things that Sarah likes. Can be awful tough sometime, getting them sent up from San Francisco."

Mackenzie spoke without looking at Bill. "I'll bring her round your store. Get Dim to pack her up sharp-like. I ain't got time for conversation."

When Mackenzie brought the dougherty back round to the post office it was packed high with bags of grain and boxes of ammunition. There was a three-foot strip free at the back.

"There's room for you," he told Marianne. After he had lifted her case there was only enough space for her to sit with her knees pulled up to her chest.

She stepped out onto the mud and slipped immediately. Mackenzie took her by her waist and lifted her the three foot to the back of the dougherty and shoved her into position. "You won't fall out," he said. "You ain't got chance to move."

Sarah came out onto the veranda. "Blankets," she said. "You will need them. The wood is awful hard and the road up to Jackson is rocky."

They packed Marianne in like fine-bone china. "Support you head," said Sarah. "It will hurt like Hell, if you let it get bumped around."

Mackenzie swung himself up to the driver's seat. Marianne heard him yaw and crack the whip. Very slowly, the wheels turned in the soft mud as the horse strained against the weight of the load. The whip cracked again and they began moving.

Marianne watched as the street rolled past and the post office receded from view. Sarah stood on the veranda, her arms were folded and slowly she too disappeared. In a few minutes the low houses of the town were replaced by temporary shacks and then smallholdings and farmland. In no time at all they had left Paradise behind them.

The dougherty followed a track cut deep into the side of the valley. Storm water bubbled and gurgled in the channels either side. The wheels splashed through puddles, throwing up plumes of brown mud. Marianne listened to Mackenzie gently talking the horse up the gradient. Maples hung over the track and there was a continual pit pat of rainwater dropping on the canvas Mackenzie had pulled over the supplies. The sun was high and light dappled through the canopy. The dougherty rocked as it made its way up the mud track washed smooth by the floodwater.

Marianne leaned her head back a roll of blanket held against the rough wooden board. Looking up, she watched the light alternate yellow and shade. She saw small birds flitted around in the branches above her. Chickadees chirped happily in the new warmth of spring and Marianne fell asleep.

The sound of Mackenzie halting the horse woke her. The dougherty abruptly halted and a tin fell cracked against Marianna's knee. It was dark and damp and the sound of rushing water filled the hollow. Marianne felt the back of neck her whole body was stiff. Mackenzie came around the back of the dougherty.

"You need to walk a part here," he said. He was wearing his leather gloves and placing one arm under her bent knees and the other around the curve her back, he plucked Marianne from where she was wedged against the stores.

"Excuse me for this," he said and set her down on. "Rain's washed away the track some. Be better if you walk it."

To the left of the track the bank was steep and water from the channel had been forced across the track, washing away the mud and cutting a diagonal gully ten-feet wide and three-foot deep.

"What do you want me to do," asked Marianne, looking at the store and cases piled high above the sides of the dougherty.

"I want you well clear. Get on my back. I'll take you across."

"I will go myself," said Marianne.

"It will knock you over," said Mackenzie. "An even if it doesn't it will soak your clothes and you to the skin. I'll not deliver you drowned or unconscious or shivering with hypothermia." He bent forward. "Place your arms around my neck."

Marianne stood were she was.

Mackenzie looked up at her and sighed. "You are a most stubborn and stupid girl. I can't think why any right-thinking man would want to take you as a wife."

Before Marianne had chance to counter, Mackenzie lunged forward, wrapped his right arm around her thighs. He raised himself and flung her over his shoulder so her head fell down over his back.

"No," protested Marianne. Mackenzie ignored her

stepped off the broken bank and plunged into the fast-flowing stream. Marianne let out a strangled cry of frustration and stared down into the dark water swirling beneath her. The blood rushed to her head and mixed with her fury. Though it took Mackenzie only four strides before he stepped clear and back onto track again, the water had come over his boots and he was quite drenched.

Marianne flattened down her hair. "I am not used to being manhandled in this manner," she said. Mackenzie winced as he straightened.

"You may have to get used to it," he said. Marianne watched him limp as he re-crossed the stream.

He climbed up into the seat, took the reins and braced his boot against the footboard. "Come on, then Bess," he said and gave the reins a light pull. The horse lifted its legs but moved not an inch forward. "Come on, Bessie." Lightly, he flicked the whip and Bess rolled her head. He cooed and coaxed her and slowly the horse took the strain and the dougherty rattled forward. Bess stepped off the bank and pressed her hooves into the water.

When Bess was in the center of the stream and the water was splashing around her flanks the front wheels teetered on the drop. Mackenzie had pulled her round so the dougherty would approach the bank square on. But still, one wheel fell first and for a moment the whole dougherty leaned sickening to one side, the bags and boxes swayed drunkenly to the edge.

Marianne felt her stomach lurch with it. Bess snorted as the she was pulled across and her eyes stared in fear. Then the other wheel fell and the dougherty righted itself. Bess reached the other side and Mackenzie cracked the whip and bade her to push up the bank. That she did and again the dougherty lurched then righted itself.

"There's no need for you to get down," Marianne said. "I am capable of getting up myself."

Mackenzie watched her as she walked past and disappeared behind the stacked boxes. The back of the dougherty was a good four-feet off the ground. Marianne lifted her boot up and tried to pull herself up, before slipping back down.

"Are you on?" asked Mackenzie.

"One moment, Mr. Mackenzie," she replied. There was nothing for to get a grip of. She pressed her hands down onto the edge and pulled herself onto her stomach. Her feet came off the ground and she pivoted on the edge of the wagon, neither on nor off.

"Now?" called Mackenzie.

"Nearly," she said, feeling the air squeezed out of her. She flailed one leg and managed to catch the back wheel with her boot. Carefully, she managed to get a toehold on a spoke and give herself enough leverage to push herself up. She fell face first and as her leg swung round she cracked her kneecap on the underside of the dougherty.

"Ready," she called, keeping the pain out of her voice.

They moved on. The gradient increased and often Marianne heard the whip crack and Mackenzie yaw as the horse struggled. There were firs; red firs and white firs and they grew close together and dizzyingly tall. Marianne gazed up at them. They spiked the blue sky and shut out much of the light. It was quiet in the pine forest with only the rattle of wheels and the constant crack of hooves. The air was cold and she wrapped her arms around her legs, piling as many blankets on top of her as she could.

They past white boulders covered with moss and small waterfalls, everywhere melt water rushed down through the forest. The track narrowed and began to turn tightly as it made its way up. There was no mud on the track now, only loose stone and the dougherty bounced wildly. Marianne's head was knocked back and forth against the wooden panels and she tried her best to cushion herself with the blankets. Very often, something would fall from the store and she would instinctively put her hand over to protect her damaged knee.

Soon, they came to smooth bare rock and the horse was slipping and Mackenzie calling to her and applying the break to stop them sliding back. They stopped beneath a large limestone boulder. Mackenzie dismounted.

"I'll lead her though the pass," he said to Marianne. He held out his arm and she took it and helped herself down. Behind them the track twisted white down through the darkness of the forest. At this height the trees were thinned out and she could see through them and down into the valley. There were subtle shades of green as the trees changed and the land fell down away from them. Somewhere down there was Paradise. In the distance she could make out a shard of brilliant blue surrounded by all that green – the lake where she had been the day before already seemed like another lifetime.

"Don't loiter behind the wagon," said Mackenzie. "If it slips back you'll be crushed."

Her joints were all cramped from how she had sat and the cold had stiffened her. Here, where it was exposed the wind blew through the pines stung her exposed skin. She walked awkwardly, holding a blanket over her head. Mackenzie led the horse, walking next to her, talking constantly into her ear.

The track curled round between the boulder and another huge rock. It was barely wide enough for the dougherty and Marianne had to claw at the rock face to pull herself up. The track was limestone, polished smooth by wind and rain and snow. The sound of hooves trying to grip made Marianne's skin prickle.

"Come on," Mackenzie said, raising his voice. The horse reared her head. Mackenzie pulled the guide rope over his shoulder and leaned into it, using his weight as best he could to pull down the horse's head and press them forward.

Marianne pressed herself against the stone wall. "What can I do?"

"Get out of the way," shouted Mackenzie. She scrambled up the slope and in twenty yards she was at the top looking back down on them.

Mackenzie drove his knees forwards, leaning 'til he was almost parallel to the incline. Marianne could see his face twist in pain. The dougherty wheels seemed to stop turning and she felt she would see them slide back, man horse and cart crash down the hill and all she could do was stand and watch them.

But they got some traction and slowly the wheels began to move again. She could see the harness pulling heavily on the horse, but the muscles moved beneath it and they pressed on up the slope. Mackenzie was level with her, his face red, both he and the horse breathing heavily.

"Keep moving," he said. "A little further."

They were on a flat, open clearing. The cool wind took away the smell of horse sweat. The track was springy moss and they followed it down and around an outcrop of rocks and into the lea of the wind. There were piles of hard-packed snow in the shade and pools of water in the sun. Dragonflies dipped low and zoomed off into the pines.

"We'll rest here a short while," said Mackenzie. He unharnessed the horse and let her water and graze the fresh shoots of grass.

"This is Pine Ridge," he said. "Behind us is Paradise. And out there," he said, indicating to where Marianne was gazing, "out there is Thunder Valley."

The valley was smaller than the one they had climbed out of. It gently shelved down in smooth folds, like a blanket unfurling. On the northern slopes the white of snow glistened. The high slopes were covered in woodland which gave way to lush grassland that waited, emerald and untouched in the spring sunshine.

"My God," said Marianne.

Mackenzie had taken a basket from beneath his seat and set it down on a rock in the sunshine. He unpacked a piece of bread, tomatoes, cheese and cold meat. Tearing a piece of meat and pushing it into a hunk of bread he said, "Old man Jackson will own most of what you see. That's what he'll say. Won't find many who'd argue with him. Not amongst the living, anyway."

They ate, enjoying the warmth of the sun as it reflected from the rock behind them. It was quite, apart from the constant grazing of the horse and the occasional cooing of doves. Mackenzie handed her a cloth and she wiped her mouth and hands and brushed the crumbs from her coat. She handed it back and Mackenzie folded it, very deliberately.

"Jackson is a hard man," he said. "Lives out here and for the most part keeps himself to himself. Pays his dues and does his trade. But them that know him, say he's a hard man."

He placed the cloth back in the basket.

"We can go back," he said. "We can go back and I'll set you on the steamer back for Sacramento. I'll deal with Jackson, you don't need to worry about that."

Marianne looked down across the valley. A breeze blew a strand of hair back and forth across her forehead and she flicked it away.

"No," she said.

"I know you're headstrong and I won't argue with you. But sometimes it ain't a bad thing to change your mind."

"I gave my word," said Marianne.

"That maybe, but I don't believe you were in a position to give your word. They have a saying round here; you have to see before you buy. Do you understand?"

"I have nothing else." Marianne said.

"There are a thousand men in Sacramento who would marry you tomorrow," said Mackenzie. "A thousand more in San Francisco."

"I gave my word," said Marianne. "It is my honor."

Mackenzie nodded. "As you wish."

He packed the leftover food into the basket and stood.

"We'll be going now then," he said. "I'll help you

onto the wagon. Looks like you took a knock to your knee."

He re-harnessed the horse and coming round to the side of the dougherty he pointed to something down in the mud.

"See that?" he asked and held hand over the print. "A big one." He straightened himself slowly. "They say the wolves grow big in Thunder Valley. I don't recommend going for any midnight promenades."

The way was easier on this side of the valley head and the track wound smoothly through pockets of Sugar Maple and Boxelder. Between the trees grew clumps of baneberry and common yarrow. Marianne shut her eyes and tried to find comfort in the assortment of blankets. But her knee pained her and sleep would not come. She sat awake rocking listlessly and listened to insects hum in the afternoon warmth.

The dougherty shook to a halt and Marianne found herself in a clearing. It was very quiet and Marianne has the impression she had awoken in another place. There was something unusual that she couldn't quite discern. Mackenzie got down and stretched his sore muscles. He helped her down and watched as she rubbed her knee.

"A bruise," she said. "Nothing more."

Lift filtered into the clearing as if through a high church window. Marianne had the impression they were very small in an enormous landscape.

"The trees," she said, looking up. Huge trunks towered upwards like Gothic stone pillars, so high she could not see where they ended.

Mackenzie nodded. "That's a lot of timber," he

said.

Marianne walked to the nearest trunk and touched it lightly. It was the color of stone and though it was hard it was not cold, as she expected, but warm from the sun. She pressed her palms against it and it seemed to vibrate with life. She let her face fall against it and instinctively tried to wrap her arms around it. She laughed at how little of the tree she could hold. It was like holding onto a giant. One of hundreds and hundreds of giants that stood waiting in rows behind.

"We need to push on," said Mackenzie. He motioned to the bridge up ahead. "She's steep. I don't want to lose you or anything else of the wagon. Walk behind, if you please, and check nothing falls."

Marianne lingered for a second and patted the tree. The bridge crossed a creek that flung itself angrily out of the forest before widening and turning slowly to run along the valley floor. The bridge was just two ramps joined by a flat bed made of wood barely wide enough for the dougherty. Marianne walked behind as Mackenzie started the horse to clop carefully up the steep incline. The front wheels of the dougherty hit the ramp and the cargo slid backwards testing the strapping and bulging against the tarpaulin.

"Is it well-enough?" shouted Mackenzie.

"Well-enough," replied Marianne.

The wooden slats were little more that loosely lay across the supports of the bridge and they moved as the wheels of the dougherty turned upon them. The horse had its ears pricked to the white-water of the river below and it didn't like the movement of the slats on its hooves. The dougherty swayed uneasily.

"Halt," shouted Marianne. One back wheel had slipped off the edge and was spinning hopelessly in open air. Marianne could see the back axle bend and tense, sickeningly. "The wheel," she said.

Mackenzie twisted in his seat and she heard him curse under his breath. He shook the reins. "Come now, Bessie," he said. "Just a few more steps." He spoke to the horse, soothing her, asking her to walk the six-feet further to the edge of the ramp.

"It's no good," he said. "She's got the fear. I can't spook her. If she starts, she'll send us all into the river."

He slowly stood from his seat, the dougherty wobbled and blew air from her nostrils. "Damn it," Mackenzie said. "I dare not leave the reins. Won't take a rabbit fart to send her off running at the moment." He sat back down.

Marianne took off her boots and climbed the ramp in her stocking feet. Carefully, she clambered under the rear axle. The loose slats wobbled as she moved on her hands and knees, pain shooting up when she pressed on her injury. She tried not to look through the large gaps and blocked out the noise of the river rushing below. On her stomach she squeezed beneath the front axle.

"For God's sake," she heard Mackenzie mutter.

Marianne edged around to the left of the four hooves planted on the bridge. Slowly, she got to her feet, feeling every creak in the wood beneath her. The horse flicked its head.

Gently, very gently, Marianne ran her fingers along its flank. She felt the skin tighten beneath her. She ran her left hand to the horse's neck then did the same with her right. She stepped closer and calmly spoke.

"Mon cher cheval, se il vous plaît ne vous

inquiétez pas," she told it. "Nous allons marcher de ce pont. Il ne est pas besoin d'avoir peur."

She ran her left hand down to the neck again, and her right hand followed. This time her right hand took the halter. She turned her shoulders so they were square to the end of the bridge and waited for the horse to focus in the same direction.

"Allez," she said, and moved forward. The horse tensed and stood its ground. Quickly, she jabbed her shoulder into the horse's neck. Unbalanced, the horse took an involuntary step to the side, as it did Marianne strode forward and the horse followed. She kept and even pace and pressed her elbow into the next to keep it straight.

Behind her, she could feel the dougherty creaking forward and Mackenzie turning his chair, trying to watch the back wheels. She paid them no heed and concentrated on the end of the bridge. As they got to the ramp she could feel the pull to her left where the back wheel was dropping below the edge of the bridge. She pressed her elbow into the horse and pushed it over to the right. Sensing the grass ahead of it the horse reached, but she held it back and took it slowly down the ramp. The dougherty wheel swung down and landed with a bump on the grassy river bank.

Marianne stood on the soft grass patted the horse on the nose. "Bonne fille," she said.

Mackenzie got down and picked up a sack of corn that had been thrown into the reeds. He looked at Marianne. "I'll get your boots," he said.

Marianne brushed down her dresses. Splinters of wood were caught in her stockings and she threw them to the ground.

"You can take the reins," said Mackenzie. "I need to walk."

"Is it bad?" Marianne asked, looking at his leg.

"No," he said. "The War. A long time ago." And he turned and walked on ahead, taking off his hat and holding it in one hand and holding a bull rush in the other.

Sitting up at the front, the reins in her hands and the horse trotting steadily in front of her, Marianne saw the whole valley open up before of her. The track followed the river, always keeping it in sight as it wended aimlessly along the wide valley bottom.

To one side, the wooded valley side ended in thick banks of brambles, barberries and cotoneasters. To the other, the reeds and rushes grew tall and occasional willows dipped their branches into the sluggish water. Across the river the reeds seemed to extend for miles, turning into countless varieties of long grasses all rippling in the gentle breeze. Flies buzzed constantly, and the horse swished its tail. Mackenzie kept ahead, striding out at a constant pace, swatting insects with his hat.

They passed a deep scar cut in to the forest where the huge trees had been felled. Marianne gazed in horrified wonder at the decapitated trunks. The stumps they left where the size of giant dining tables. Here, the forest was silent and empty.

Without warning Mackenzie turned, taking a track that almost doubled-back into the forest. It led into a large circular clearing, like a huge green lagoon cut into the surrounding forest. There were a number of outbuildings, stables and a large farmhouse, all built with wooden boards and painted dark red. The ranch house had two floors with verandas under a wide-sweeping roof.

A man was working in the stables and he stopped to watch them. Mackenzie raised his hat to him. "The Chinaman is Lou," he said. "You need not worry about him. Bring her round in front of them outhouses there."

Lou stood watching them with his hands on his hips, the late afternoon sun shining on his face. "Mac," he said, walking over and nodding at Mackenzie. "Wasn't sure you'd make it today with the rain and all."

"Wasn't so bad," replied Mackenzie. "The boss man around?"

"Huntin'," said Lou, his gaze fixed on Marianne.

"This here is Marianne," said Mackenzie. Marianne got down from the seat and took her boots from Mackenzie.

"Yes, I see," said Lou, stroking his chin. "Pleasure to make your acquaintance."

"Likewise," said Marianne, as she put on her boots.

"Well, these pleasantries are sure nice, but I need be making a sharp turnaround, if I'm going to make Paradise by tonight. If you take care of your guest, Lou, I'll tip your supplies."

"There's a guestroom made up at the back of the house," said Lou. "Housekeeper has the soap and hot water ready."

Mackenzie unloaded the supplies into the outhouse. Lou took Marianne's case.

"I can take it," said Marianne. Lou ignored here. A woman stood on the veranda. She was a short woman, severe with small, black eyes.

"This is Ola," said Lou.

"Follow me," instructed Ola.

It was dark inside and smelt of bitter polish. Ola climbed the staircase and led Marianne to a large bedroom. It was light inside, a large window opened out onto the upstairs veranda. There was a bed, a large closet, a chest of drawers and a full-length mirror. Ola shut the curtains and opened a side door. Inside a small room was a large copper bathtub.

"You need to wash," said Ola. "I will bring you towels and hot water."

Marianne took her shoes off and sat on the bed. Ola came with a large stack of white towels and then with a steaming jug of water. It took six trips before the tub was two-thirds full and the room was thick with mist.

"Where are my things?" asked Marianne.

"You do not need them," said Ola. She opened the closet and one of the drawers. They were full of clothes, very fine clothes. "These are for you."

"I don't understand."

"You," Ola said, pointing at Marianne, "wear these clothes."

"But the size?" asked Marianne.

"You wrote with your measurements," said Ola. "They were correct?"

"Yes."

The woman appraised Marianne with pursed lips. "Well, these clothes will fit you."

"What about my things?"

"You must wash," said Ola. "Dinner is in two hours." She closed the door behind her.

A terrible weariness spread over Marianne. She sat on the bed and for a moment she thought she might cry. No, she had not done that before now, and she would not be starting. She must do what she had to do. She needed to remove her dirty clothes and she badly needed a wash.

She pulled off her boots and undid her hair. Then she unzipped her dress, slipped it off her shoulders. It was so stiff with grime that she could just step out of it, as if stepping out of her barrel. She rolled down her stockings and threw them onto the pile. They smelt of many months of the road, boat and rail. The dirty clothes seemed to contaminate the room and she felt obliged to kick them into a corner.

In the bathroom she breathed in the hot air. The steam felt good on her body. She took off her underwear, but it too seemed to be an aberration in the room and she walked back into the bedroom and threw them into the pile. As she did she caught sight of herself in the mirror and was momentarily captivated by the image of her own nakedness. She paused. She hadn't looked at herself for many months.

Her skin was very white in the darkness of the room. Her face had caught the sun a little and her neckline was visible. She had lost weight and her bones were visible, her color, her ribs and painfully her hips. Her breasts were yet smaller and she wrapped them in her arms. An angry mark violated her knee. Self-consciousness reclaimed her and she quickly tiptoed back into the bathroom.

She caught her breath as she slipped into the hot water. After so long cramped on hard wooden seats, the sensation as her muscles unwound almost made he feint. The tub was deep and she felt her body rise to the surface, as if a piece of driftwood. She felt her knee and the insect bites and a hundred other nicks and scuffs her body had endured. And then she felt nothing as a certain numbness came over her.

She thought of Mackenzie and how they had not said goodbye. She thought of his
war wound and how he would get the horse and wagon back safely in the descending darkness. She though of Sarah and the look on her face and they had left the post office in Paradise. And she thought of other acquaintances she had made, faces and voices that had come momentarily into her life on boats and steam carriages and left, and then past, blurring into one image of humanity. And she thought of nothing, her brain tired of thinking and her legs floating to the surface.

The bedroom door opened with a long-drawn out creak. She started.

"Hello," she said. For a moment she thought it was maybe a sudden breeze. Then she heard footsteps. They trod softly on the floorboards, but with a solidity of purpose and she could sense their weight. "Hello," she repeated. "Lou?"

She turned to look through the narrow gap where she had not closed the door properly. The figure moved in the room and cast a shadow as it passed the door and then again as it passed back. The door closed again with a creak. She sunk back into the water and she knew who it was and that he was showing her that he would do as he liked with her. She would not relax, so she scrubbed herself with the hard block of yellow soap. Scrubbed herself harshly as if it were a purge.

She dried herself standing in the tub then stepped out onto a towel. She wrapped a towel around her and opened the bedroom curtains a touch to let a little light into the room and saw that a dress was lying on the bed. Everything had been picked out for her down to the white lace underwear and a pair of shoes at the foot of the bed.

The dress was a deep green, the color of the new shoots of grass up on the ridge. It hung from her shoulders a little. In the drawers she found some tissue paper and folding it she successfully padded out her brassiere. There was also a jewelry box and she found a set of earrings and a brooch all inlaid with jade. She rested them in her hands for a while, feeling their weight. Though she held them in her hand they did not seem real, she could not tell whether she liked them and lost all sense of what they signified.

Her hair was matted from the soapy water and fell down in great wet ringlets. She opened the door and stood on the veranda. She toweled her hair and looked out over the stone remains of old buildings, covered by creeping nature. In one a young sapling grew out of the center and through where the roof had been. Behind her the sun was low and it illuminated the hillside in front. The trees banked up in multitudes of color. At the very top she could make out the crags of Pine Ridge, outlined against a darkening sky.

She tied up her hair and put on the earrings. In the drawer was an alabaster jar of very expensive perfume. She applied it to her neck and her wrists where she could feel the pulse. It smelt wrong, as if it had been kept in the drawer too long and spoiled. She stepped into the shoes, went downstairs and walked out of the house. She crossed the dirt yard, went past the stables, and walked through the long grass towards the river. All the time she felt eyes on the back of her head, watching her as she went.

She stood at the river, watching it swirl lazily. It was cold, clear melt-water from the snow on the peaks and Marianne could see trout pointed upstream, feeding on the gravel bottom. Across the river the valley lay verdant and shimmering. She felt as if she could walk into it, disappear and never return.

As she looked she made out tiny, dark shapes against green. Whether they were trees, people, animals or some other structure, she could not tell. She looked at them until they seemed to move and she was not sure whether it was them or her vision that was failing her.

"Miss Marianne," said Lou and she jumped. "You must come to the house."

Ola waited on the veranda and said. "Is it normal for you to go wandering wherever you please?"

"I wandered halfway round the world to get here," said Marianne.

She followed Ola along the veranda and into the end room. It was a dining room, the depth of the whole house. The end was open to the evening and looked out over a bending old Black Oak.

Ola directed her down the length of the long, narrow dining table. "Here," she said, pointing to the chair at the far end. Marianne sat. The chairs were very hard and upright and were not meant for feeling comfortable.

Marianne looked out at the squat, old oak. The last of the sunlight catching its new, budding-leaves. Between two low branches a hammock had been slung and a little further up a rope swing hung, motionless and empty.

Marianne regarded them with interest as a large bee flew the room with a heavy drone. Ola busied herself and Lou could be heard, tramping about the veranda. Marianne very mush wished she were outside and lying in the long grass.

Lou struggled with a set of panels and leaned them against the corner post. He held a panel on the outside and without speaking Ola brought the bolts across from the inside and fastened it in. Like this they moved around the exterior wall, blocking in the room, one panel at a time.

Marianne sat and watched as the shadow they cast came slowly along the table towards her. Before the last panel was put in place, she caught a last glance of the swing begin to move in an evening breeze. Then, the room was in darkness.

Ola came with a candle and lit the oil lamps and the odor of sperm whale oil mixed with Marianne's perfume. She watched Ola set the table and for a moment she felt as if she were back in the hold of the boat. And then, Ola left and Marianne waited on her own.

He opened the door and stood at the end of the table looking down at her. "Marianne," he said, "I'm William Jackson."

He was a broad man but not overweight. His hair and beard were cropped close to his face in a way that seemed to project the hardness of his features. His face was worn by the elements. The lamplight highlighted his wrinkles and shone in eyes that were very alive and regarded Marianne with a slow-burning intensity. His hand rested on the back of a chair. He had big hands, strong and powerful and Marianne wondered about them.

Marianne knew she should get up but felt herself pressed into her chair. Jackson didn't move but stood there looking at her.

"It's a great pleasure to meet you," she said. The words sounded empty and insufficient.

"Your room," he said. "I trust it is all to your satisfaction."

She nodded in reply.

"I see you have found the clothes," he said. "The color, I think, suits you very well. I recalled you had communicated that your eyes too were green," he offered in explanation. "The perfume also. It was a favorite of my wife's. My late wife's, you understand."

She nodded again and he was about to say something more when Ola entered carrying bowls of food.

"Should I serve?" she asked.

"Yes," said Jackson, taking his seat. He motioned her forward. "Please do."

Ola served the food, careful not to look at either of them and nobody spoke.

"And the wine," said Jackson. "Please bring the wine."

She came back with a decanter filled with ruby-colored wine. Jackson tasted it. "Yes," he said. "Yes, indeed. Will you take some wine Marianne? I must apologize; it is not French. But we have some passable wines produced here in California. They are much improved, I believe."

Ola poured a little into her glass. "Mixed with water?" she inquired.

"No," said Marianne.

When Ola left the room, Jackson picked up his cutlery, paused and said. "Since my wife died I've been out of the habit of saying grace. Perhaps you'd like to give thanks before we eat."

"I am most grateful to you, Mr. Jackson," said Marianne. "But I think I'm too hungry to do anything but eat."

Jackson smiled. "I am sure," he said. "Let's eat."

Marianne ate mechanically, barely conscious of the food she consumed. She listened to the clatter and scrape of metal and porcelain and marveled that anyone could eat without speaking in such a way. The silence was broken by the sudden buzzing of the bee, which appeared to have been put to sleep by the quiet darkness. They watched as it flew around the room, casting huge confusing shadows on all four walls simultaneously.

Ola entered carrying a fly swat and Marianne realized she must have been outside the door listening.

"Wait," Jackson told her. "No need to kill it. Bees do as much work on this ranch as you do." He took an empty glass and serviette and carefully directed the bee into one other with the other. It gave an angry muffled buzz and fell silent. Jackson opened the door and tipped the bee out onto the handrail of the veranda. Before he closed the door again, Marianne saw the bee fly towards the river in a big, lazy loop.

"They pollinate the crops," explained Jackson.

"I know," said Marianne. "Which crops do you grow?"

Jackson seemed surprised she was interested. "What do you think?"

"I've seen berries," said Marianne. "Lots of

berries. And you could grow apples," she said. "The land looks right for an orchard. And grains, I suppose. Maize and barley."

Jackson looked at her over the rim of his wine glass. "Yes," he said. He considered for a moment. "It is mainly timber," he said. "But I believe one day we will cultivate oranges, prunes, plums, grapes, figs, apricots, almonds, walnuts, olives, and lemons."

Marianne frowned. "Its too cold," she said.

"Here, yes. But further down the valley it is very sheltered. You'd be surprised," he said. "The difficulty is transporting the produce out of here. We are rather isolated, here in our valley. But, of course, you have seen that today."

He sipped his wine.

"I suspect," he continued, "that this last leg may not have been the most arduous of your journey."

"It was long," said Marianne. "But I am here now."

"Indeed," said Jackson. They continued the rest of their meal in silence.

When they had finished and Ola had cleared away the plates, Jackson took a desert wine and held it to the light to contemplate it.

"You understand, I think, the terms of our arrangement," he said.

"I believe it is quite clear," she replied.

"So, you can confirm that your father received one-third of the amount agreed upon when he and you signed and sent our agreement?"

"That is correct," said Marianne.

"And now, because you have arrived here, on the date we agreed, that I am now at liberty to authorize my agent in France to release to your father the second third."

"I would be most grateful to you, if you could," said Marianne.

"Of course," said Jackson. "I will instruct it tomorrow."

"I don't mean to appear to doubt you," said Marianne, "but how would I receive confirmation of the payment?"

Jackson nodded. "You are right to be thorough in business. There are many men who would seek to dupe you. I will ask for your father's signature to be sent as confirmation for you to witness."

Marianne nodded. "And the third payment?"

"That will be completed the day following our wedding. And with that my financial dealings with your father will be complete."

"What if we do not marry?"

"I would not pay the money."

"The final third?"

"Yes."

"And the first two?"

"They would already have been paid."

"And you would not propose to reclaim the payments?"

"I do not believe there is any way I could do that. I presume that we intend to honor our arrangements."

Marianne nodded. "The money will make a big difference to my father," she said. Jackson gave no indication that he wished her to continue but she did so anyway.

"My brother would like to become an engineer. He is clever, I think."

"And your father," asked Jackson, "what does he

do?"

"He does not work. He used to make watches but now his eyes are failing him. He had to sell his business. We live mainly off the proceeds of the sale."

"I see," said Jackson. "And do you have any other siblings?"

"My sister, Chloe."

"Does she work?"

"She cannot work," said Marianne. She held a piece of tablecloth in her hand and looked at it. "She has health problems. My father must care for her, you understand."

"And your mother?"

"She is dead."

"I see," said Jackson, plainly. "I would like to smoke a cigar on the veranda. Please join me."

Marianne was astonished to see there was still light in the evening. It had felt as though she had been in the room for hours and almost wondered whether it wasn't morning. She stood next to Jackson and though he leaned on the rail and she was wearing the shoes, she was still barely as tall as his shoulder. Jackson lit his cigar and breathed out its rancid smoke.

"My wife, as you know, died five years ago."

Marianne nodded.

"She died in childbirth."

Marianne felt a jolt and held the handrail also. "I am very sorry," she said with feeling. "It is a terrible tragedy, to lose a wife and baby also."

Jackson blew out the purple cigar smoke. "We were lucky," he said. "With God's will, Thomas survived."

"Pardon?" said Marianne, staring to look at him.

"Yes," he said, nodding and tapping the cigar against the rail. "He survived and grew strong."

"You have a child?"

"No," Jackson laughed. "I have six. How could I live here without my children?"

"Six children," said Marianne, raising her voice. "No, this is not possible."

"Of course," said Jackson. "This was all made clear by either me or my agent."

"No, I did not know," said Marianne. "I did not know."

Ola appeared beside them. "Should I clear the table?"

Jackson nodded his assent. "You will meet them soon enough," he said. "They have been out in the fields all afternoon. Good for them to be out. They have been inside most of the winter." He ducked down beneath the rail and jumped to the ground. "Come on," he called behind him, "we'll see if they are approaching."

Marianne followed and they walked to the river. The sun had set behind the far mountains and the valley was in gray shadow. Jackson took big strides and Marianne had to skip to keep up. Jackson threw his cigar stub to the ground and stood on the bank.

"Can you see them?" he asked, peering through the darkness. "Your eyes are no doubt better than mine."

A low mist clung to the long grass and at first Marianne saw nothing. Then slowly she made out shapes moving towards them.

"Yes, I see," she said. "A horse rider and a wagon."

"Good," said Jackson. "That will be William

Junior on the horse, he is nearly 20. Edward and Elizabeth will be driving the wagon. They are twins."

"Twins," said Marianne.

"16 years old. Both look like their mother."

As she watched the horse rider materialized. She could see the nonchalant way he rode and the way he wore his hat. The wagon came very slowly as if it bore a heavy weight.

"There are others too, walking beside the wagon."

"That will be Emily," said Jackson. "She is 12 and tall and skinny though she eats more than I do. Robert, he is 10. And, of course, Thomas. Poor, little man. They made him walk all that way."

They came, emerging like a clan through the gloom. William Junior waved his hat and Jackson waved back and someone hollered from the wagon. She could hear them chattering and laughing and felt a rising wave of fear and panic.

"No," she said. "I cannot."

The horse splashed down into the river and William Junior directed the wagon over the natural ford. Marianne heard a shriek and saw Robert run and plunge himself into water. Emily picked up Thomas and waded across. And it seemed they were all upon her. Marianne turned and fled, losing her shoes halfway between the river and the house. She saw the blurred image of Lou and Ola watching her as she ran inside. She fell onto the bed and cried, cried a long time before she really understood why.

In the morning Jackson left a pot of coffee, oranges, and warm bread by the door. He knocked and went away. He came back forty minutes later, knocked again and this time entered. Marianne sat on the bed. Jackson opened the curtains letting in bright sunlight. He took an orange from the tray, stood by the window and started peeling it. Marianne could hear the sound of children playing outside.

"I am sorry," said Marianne. "A shock."

"I have never been to Europe," said Jackson. "I traveled to Mexico City once to buy horses." He shook his head at the memory.

"It's not that," said "Marianne. "I like it here." She looked down at her hands. "My mother died when my sister was born. Ten years ago. My father and me." She looked around the room, helplessly. "It destroyed us."

Jackson sucked on a piece of orange. "I see," he said.

"I cannot be a mother to these children," said Marianne. "I cannot."

Jackson laughed. "They are a handful. But I am not asking you to do that. They can look after themselves."

"They will not accept me."

"They know you will be good for me. And if they don't know now, they will learn." He turned from the window. "But I will not keep you here. Anytime you wish to leave, just say. William Junior will take you back to Paradise." He left the room, closing the door softly behind him.

Marianne breathed deeply. She did not give in and she would not give in now. Her father would get the money he deserved, all the money. She got out of bed and shouted down for Ola to bring her some water.

THE END

Mail Order Bride: Three English Sisters, One Cowboy & The Navajo Nation

Synopsis: Mail Order Bride: Three English Sisters, One Cowboy & The Navajo Nation - Three sisters from London strike out for the Americas, where one already has a fiancé in waiting – a cowboy in Nevada. He knows that two other women are coming but doesn't know what he'll quite do with them when they arrive. They garner plenty of attention from the other men in town and soon, the cowboy finds that his small house has become crowded as he and his new bride seek a little bit of privacy to start their lives.

"Oh my dear baby sister. My dear misguided Andrea. How many women doctors do you know of? And where would you get the money to attend college? And lastly – are your grades even good enough to enable you to get into a medical college?"

Andrea was close to tears as she listened to her eldest sister Chloe explain why her dream was frivolous and would never be realized.

She stopped washing the breakfast dishes and asked, "Well, if you are running off to America to marry that cowboy, what is to become of me and Margaret?"

"We've been over this numerous times, you two are coming with me and we will find you suitable husbands and you will live a happy life."

"It all sounds so easy when you say it. Especially when you say it so quickly, like it's a walk down the street. You are dragging us half way around the world."

"But I must warn you, it won't be easy, you are rather hideous," Chloe joked, ignoring Andrea's protestations.

Her sixteen-year-old sister was at the age where vanity ruled her life and found that she could not pass a mirror or a shop window without checking her appearance.

Andrea yelped and threw a wet dishrag at Chloe.

The other sister, the eighteen-year-old Margaret, was anything but careful with her appearance. Her mind always seemed to be miles away, thinking about what – heaven only knew. She was forever writing - she had notebooks filled with her thoughts and stories, but never showed them to anyone. As to reading – she was a voracious reader; knowledgeable on any topic that one would care to discuss. If the family needed to know anything, they would ask Margaret. She was, their father used to say, a living library.

The sisters had been left on their own after their parents had succumbed, within days of each other, to influenza a couple of years prior and it fell to Chloe, being the oldest, to look after them. Their father had left them a small inheritance, enough to get by on for a while, but the time had come when the money was running out and something had to be done to secure their future.

Chloe was taking them to America. She had started a relationship, by post, with a young cowboy in New Mexico and although she had only seen pictures of him, she was deeply in love. They had been corresponding for over a year and knew each other well. Well enough to be married, they felt.

But Chloe could not leave her sisters behind. They had to come along as there was to be no future for the younger girls should she leave them in London. She was torn, Andrea had a quick mind and had done well in her studies and perhaps she could very well have become a doctor. But it was not possible financially.

And Margaret, well Margaret would starve to death – not for lack of food, but she would, no doubt, forget to eat and die. Her body would be found weeks later half eaten by rats. No, she had to come along; perhaps there would be a cowboy for her -- or a nunnery. It was a pity they weren't Catholic.

She had promised them that if they came to hate America, or were terribly homesick, they could return to England.

Chloe's betrothed, Bill Butler, had been the one to suggest she bring her sisters along. He claimed there were cowboys enough for all the unwed women in England should they so desire to come to the land of the free. It was this suggestion that first gave Chloe some hope for her sisters' future. Even if they could not find husbands, at least the newlyweds would be nearby to look after them.

While Andrea's dream of becoming a doctor would have to remain a dream, Bill had assured her that there was always a demand for nurses should she wish to pursue a career in the medical profession.

Chloe knew this responsibility would be tough on her marriage but she had faith that love would see them through. It took some convincing, but Andrea and Margaret finally agreed that a move would be best for all concerned – although Andrea was still fighting it tooth and nail.

Agreement secured, Chloe went ahead and made plans for the journey and they were set.

On their third day out at sea, the girls strolled the deck arm in arm chatting about the adventure they were embarking on.

"Well there is a college by the name of Harvard that is supposed to be the best in the land, but Andrea dear I don't think that is realistic."

"And why not? You promised me that you would do your best to see that I get a chance at becoming a doctor. You said that women in America didn't take whatever role was assigned to them. You said that women in America were strong."

"Now dear, I did not say anything about being a doctor, what I said was -- a job in the medical profession. Such as a nurse. As usual, you stopped listening to me once you had heard what you wanted to hear."

"Nurse! I could have stayed in London and become a nurse. Easily!"

"Yes, but you would have been all alone. I promised mother and father that you and Margaret would be looked after. This is my way of looking after you. For pity's sake Andrea, I'm doing the best I can with what I have. Let's just be happy that we aren't living on the streets. Because that is where we were heading. And you know what happens to destitute girls living in East London."

"Are you saying I would have become a prostitute?"

"Yes, that is precisely what I am saying. Either a prostitute or a barmaid. And there isn't much difference between the two. Now why don't we put all this behind us and just enjoy what we have now. There will be time enough to worry about the future when it arrives. Besides you're upsetting Margaret."

On hearing her name Margaret said, "I'm sorry, where you talking to me? I wasn't paying attention I'm afraid. My mind was elsewhere."

"No dear, we were just chatting about the future, talking about what we were going to do once we are in New Mexico. And what kind of husbands we might find for you two."

Margaret frowned and shook her head, "I don't want a husband. Why would I want a husband? I have you two."

Andrea joined in, "That's all well and good for now. But there will come a time when you want something more. Haven't you ever thought about what you want for your life? They say that America is the land of opportunity. Anything is possible. Even becoming a doctor, right Chloe?"

"Shhh. I said we've had enough of the doctor talk for now."

Margaret smiled, "She just wants to be a doctor because she has an unhealthy interest in blood. Did you see what she did to the neighbor boy's poor frog?

That gave me nightmares for a week, I tell you."

Andrea shook her head and said, "We said we would never speak of that incident again."

"Well if I can't be with you two for the rest of my life, I rather think I should like to live with the Navajo. Maybe I can find a Navajo husband and live in a teepee."

"What on earth are you prattling on about? What is a Navajo and what, pray tell, is a teepee." Chloe was bewildered by Margaret's comment. Not that she wasn't used to it, Margaret would often say something right out of the blue that would puzzle whoever happened to be listening.

"If you ever read anything other than Bill's letters, you might know that the Navajo is an Indian tribe living in New Mexico. A teepee is what they live in. A sort of tent affair made of deer skin." Margaret was proud of her knowledge but was loathe to showing it off unless the conversation called for it.

"Deer skin? That sounds fascinating," Andrea said, eyes wide open.

Chloe was appalled, "Well I think it sounds disgusting!"

"Speaking of places to live," Margaret queried, "What kind of a house does Bill have? Is there going to be enough room for us?"

"It will be big enough for now, but it is simple. Nothing fancy. He built it himself."

"And you're sure that he will be able to cope with three women? I mean, what with you two being newlyweds and all. The man must be a saint." Margaret was leery of the living arrangements.

"Oh he's a sweetheart! Wait until you meet and get to know him!"

"I feel as if I do know him. He's all you've talked about for the past year," Andrea quipped.

Ignoring Andrea's snide comment, Chloe continued, "And I'm sure he will find suitable men for you two in short order. So the living arrangements will be temporary, I'm certain of it."

A steward - a steward who had been giving them grief since they had set sail from England, interrupted them, "Hey, you girls! What have I told you about this deck? It is for the first class passengers only. Now you young ladies get back below deck with your parents. If I find you up here one more time…"

Andrea snapped, "What will you do? Throw us off in the middle of the ocean? So first class passengers are the only people privileged enough to enjoy some daylight and fresh air? They're entitled to this just because they have money? Excuse me, Mr. Steward, but air and light are free for all! And, by the way, our parents are dead!"

Chloe turned the girls around and ushered them below deck. She had grown accustomed to this, it had happened at least three times a day since they had left port.

Two weeks later the train from New York carrying the Simpson sisters pulled into Santa Fe. Waiting at the station was Bill -- and several of his cowboy friends.

The girls' arrival had been eagerly awaited by most of the single cowboys in the region. Not that they were all that anxious to find a bride and settle down, but women were something of a rarity in the territory of New Mexico and the cow hands wanted to be the first to be able to say that they had seen them.

Bill spotted Chloe long before she saw him and he raced to kiss and hug her. She was literally swept off her feet by the handsome, six-foot cowboy with the blondish hair, who spun her around until they were both dizzy. The gathered cowboys whistled and applauded and threw in the odd howl for good measure.

The raucous atmosphere and din terrified Margaret and Andrea and they stood off at the end of the platform, away from the festivities. However, it wasn't long before an observant cowboy spotted them and rushed to bid them welcome. Others followed suit and before the girls knew it, they were surrounded. This left Bill and Chloe alone to say a proper hello.

"I've dreamt of this for months now. I can't believe you are finally here. You are even more beautiful than your picture. I thought your hair was brown, but now I see it has a little red in it. And those big brown eyes, why Miss Simpson, your eyes are prettier than those of my favorite cow!"

Chloe laughed uncontrollably, unable to stop for a full minute before finally saying, "I don't know what upsets me more – the fact that you have just compared my beauty to that of livestock, or the fact that you actually have a 'favorite' cow."

"You have no idea how long I had to think about what I would say when I finally saw you face to face. Sorry, but that's the best I could come up with. Now that I think about it, I guess it is not the best thing I could have said. Okay, I think we should rescue your sisters and get along to the parson."

"Parson?"

"Yeah, he's going to marry us. He's been waiting for two days, he's very excited – he doesn't get to perform many marriage ceremonies – not much call for that in these parts. Mostly funerals."

"Well this does sound like a lovely place. And what church does the parson represent?"

"I'm not sure. To tell you the truth, we're not even sure if he's a real parson. He just showed up one day a few years back, started holding church services in the saloon on Sundays, and said he was a parson. We never had one before and nobody has complained. He seems to do a good job though. There was a rumor, when he first got here, that he had been run out of Mexico for killing someone. But there's no proof and we have no reason to think poorly of him."

"My sisters are looking very frightened."

"Yeah, those boys will do that to women. Let's go get them."

Bill and Chloe gathered up the girls, hopped onto the buckboard that Bill had travelled to the station in and made their way to the parson's house.

The ceremony lasted an hour but could have easily been accomplished in twenty minutes. The parson, however, seized on the opportunity provided by a captive congregation and delivered a fire and brimstone sermon on the evils of liquor, which, as it so happened, was a bit of a problem in the territory.

The gathered assembly then moved the

celebration to the saloon where the festivities continued until dawn. Bill and the girls however, managed to sneak off sometime shortly after nightfall and headed home. The stories coming out of the evening would entertain the community for months to come.

Chloe quickly settled into her duties as a bride and found them to be very similar to her duties as the guardian of two girls in London. The transition, it seemed, was to be much easier than she had anticipated.

Margaret and Andrea, on the other hand, were having a hard time adapting to their new frontier life. They were used to having people around.

Margaret, absolutely lost without a library nearby, had taken to spending her days writing, until she ran out of paper. She started writing in the margins of her books.

And Andrea started spending all of her time on what she called 'nature walks' – she said she wanted to survey the flora and fauna of their new home. Chloe, remembering the neighbor boy and his ill-fated frog, made sure that when she left the house she was not in possession of a knife or any sharp instrument. Bill warned her to stay far clear of the western area of the land.

"The Navajo are to the west. We have a deal with them, they leave the cattle alone and they are free to set up camp in the area. They are good neighbors and we aim to keep it that way. They actually keep watch on the herd and will come and get us if a mother cow is having a hard time giving birth. Oh, by the way, there are antelope here and you may be lucky enough to see some. It is so nice to watch them run. They're pretty graceful."

Now, Andrea had a problem with boundaries and had spent her entire life pushing and testing them. As a result, no one should have been surprised when, one quiet afternoon, she ventured near to the Navajo territory and sat in the sand behind some tumbleweed and observed the goings on in the camp. She was fascinated by what little she could see.

There definitely seemed to be an order to their society and how things were done. She had never seen anything like it in London. By all appearances, there were rules that were being followed. It seemed everyone had a job to do, even the children, they spent their days helping the women and in school. School was held outdoors and consisted of a single woman standing in the middle of a circle of children and talking.

The children listened attentively. Andrea could see no books and no one was writing. She was spellbound. She made a mental note of the time that school was in session and made every effort to be there daily so she could watch.

Margaret had finally run out of paper and was starting to eye the walls when Chloe decided to speak to Bill about it.

"Bill, dearest, can you please take Margaret into town to get some writing paper? And perhaps she can get a book or two somewhere. She needs to read. Even if it just a penny dreadful."

"What? A what? Penny dreadful?"
"Yes, they are just cheap books full of bad stories

that boys in England like, or used to like, I'm not sure if they are in fashion these days. They're rubbish really, but it is something to keep her mind engaged. They were called penny dreadful because they cost a penny and I'm sure you can guess why the word 'dreadful' was used to describe them."

"You do know we have a library don't you?"

"No! I would have never imagined that. Here?"

"Oh yes. It's not as fine as what you find in the big cities, but most folks around here seem to like it. Why don't I take her by the library."

"You are a saint. I think you've just saved our Margaret's life. Well maybe not her life, but you have definitely rescued her sanity, that much is certain."

Margaret couldn't believe that there would be a library in this backwater. But as Bill was fond of pointing out, Santa Fe was growing as rapidly as the Navajo population, which was experiencing something of a boom. There were murmurs of statehood in the not too distant future and proper lawmen. Not quite London, but now that she had a library nearby, Margaret had all she needed to be happy.

Bill and Margaret came back from town in a couple of hours and she was smiling.

It had been a long time since Chloe had seen Margaret this happy and she said, "So I am guessing from the big smile that you succeeded in getting something to read and some paper. Is that correct?"

Margaret laughed, "Oh, yes I did, and do you want to hear something funny?"

"I always want to hear something funny, you

know that!"

"The librarian is from London! She came out a few years ago; she's a schoolteacher and librarian. The library is next to the school!"

Chloe turned to Bill and asked, "You have an English librarian and school teacher and you didn't think that we would find that interesting?"

"You know what? In my defense, I've never set foot in the library until today. And when I went to school, the teacher was a very old lady from Arizona. I had no idea, you know I would have told you if I had known."

The girls were laughing with delight when Andrea arrived home to help prepare dinner. It wasn't often that Bill was around at mealtime and they had planned a big dinner for that evening. He was gone all day as a rule and sometimes would be working away from home for several days and nights taking care of cattle on some distant pasture. It was special when he was home.

Andrea surveyed the festive scene and asked, "What is the joke? What is so funny? I want to laugh too!"

They explained the reason for the laughter and made plans to visit the Madeline the librarian the first opportunity they had.

Life with the girls took on a rhythm – a routine that included shooing away cowboys. Try as he might, Bill could not keep the cowboys away from Margaret and Andrea -- they were constantly dropping by. It was quite entertaining as they managed to fabricate some very creative reasons for dropping by. Not that anyone objected to the visits, but it did tend to get a little disruptive. And the house was crowded enough, but Bill had to admit it was nice to have some male company.

Chloe and Bill were playing the role of parents and he was getting more than a little concerned. He really wanted Chloe to himself. Perhaps he was being selfish, but they were newlyweds and some privacy would have been very much appreciated. When he was building the house, he had planned for it to house him, his wife and maybe a couple of small children. Four adults in the house had not been the plan and it was crowded. He discussed his concern with Chloe.

"You know I love your sisters, right?"

"What an odd thing to say," Chloe replied, "Is there something you want to tell me? Are you planning to divorce me to marry one, or heaven forbid, both of them?"

"No, I was thinking more about maybe divorcing them."

"What? You want to toss my sisters out?"

"No, nothing like that. It's just that it is getting crowded in here -- and that's okay. But the boys are always here. Like bees to flowers. I think in order to get rid of the bees we have to move the flowers."

"That's logical, yes. Or kill the bees," she said, a broad, wicked smile on her face. The thought of these boys, or rather – men, clamoring for the attentions of her sisters had been disturbing her as well. She had been giving this a lot of thought.

Bill laughed and said, "We're not going to kill the

bees. I would love to build the girls a house of their own, but I just don't have the time right now. Any chance one or both of them might be interested in marrying one of the bees?"

"I really don't think they have given much thought to the idea. Andrea is always off on her nature walks and Margaret always has her nose buried in a book. Although I have noticed that one of your friends seems to be a bit of a reader himself. I've overhead, totally by accident of course -- I would never think of invading their privacy -- I've overheard Margaret talking with the cowboy who wears spectacles. He seems to be a bit of a reader as well. They appear to have long discussions."

"Oh yes – the Professor – we call him Professor. He likes to read."

"Well, he does seem quite taken with our Margaret."

"And how about her? Does she like him?"

"Oh who knows? Margaret doesn't talk about men. She's never shown a lot of interest, but then again, Margaret doesn't really let anyone know how she feels about anything. So she may very well like him."

"So we are now in the matchmaking business?"

"Sometimes nature needs a little help and I think I can hurry this along. For our sakes and for the sake of our flowers."

"And I'll see what I can do with the bee. You know what, let's drop this whole bee and flower thing, I feel stupid."

Chloe laughed and nodded her head, "Okay – let's get our Margaret together with the Professor."

"Good, one down and one to go. How about

Andrea?"

"Andrea is a force of nature. We're not going to do any matchmaking there. She will chose someone in her own time."

"Speaking of Andrea, do you have any idea where she goes when she is out on her 'nature walks'? She seems to be gone for an awful long time. There isn't that much to see around here."

"No she never really says much. She does tell us when she sees some antelope, but that is the extent of it I'm afraid. Why? Are you worried?"

"Not worried. Just don't want her getting lost or anything."

"Don't worry about her. She can take care of herself."

Andrea had been moving closer and closer to the Navajo as she watched the activity. She had observed what appeared to be a graduation ceremony at the 'school'. And curiously, it seemed that it was only the boys who graduated. Once they were done with the schooling, they joined the men and Andrea never saw them in the school setting again. Most interesting.

One day, as she was squatting behind a bush watching the comings and goings, she was startled by movement behind her. She turned and standing over her was the woman who had been teaching the children. The teacher had caught her spying. For once in her life she felt guilty and terrified. She wasn't really doing anything wrong but it could be classified as rude. However, she did not know how the Navajo viewed spying. And that is what she was doing. There was no other word for it.

The stern look on the woman's face told Andrea that her presence was not appreciated and she leapt to her feet and ran as fast as she could in the direction of the Navajo camp. She had been so upset that she had lost her bearings and while she realized she was traveling in the wrong direction, she could not seem to change her path. The teacher ran after her shouting something in Navajo. As she approached the first teepee on the edge of the encampment she slowed her pace, thinking to herself, "Now what do I do?"

She stopped and turned to the teacher. Tears were streaming from her eyes and all she could think of to say was, "Sorry! I'm so sorry. This is so very rude of me. Please forgive me. I won't do it anymore." She closed her eyes and waited for the worst.

But nothing happened. She heard footsteps. She slowly opened her eyes to find herself surrounded by a half dozen children and the teacher. All were smiling with the exception one little boy who was sobbing. They did not seem upset or in the least bit disturbed by her presence.

Then she fainted.

A mile or so away, Margaret was being interrogated by her sister as they sat sipping tea.

"So this man they call Professor, you two are friendly?"

"I don't know if I would say we are friendly. We do talk a lot. He likes reading and has recommended some books I might like. Our taste in literature seems to be similar. And he likes to write. So we do have a lot in common."

"Anything of a romantic nature brewing there?"

"What a strange question. Now why on earth would you ask something like that? It's not really your business now is it?"

"I'm sorry. I don't mean to pry. But when we were in London, talking about coming over here, we did discuss the possibility of you finding someone to marry. I was wondering how that was going. Do you still think it is time for you to start thinking of a husband?"

"Of course. But let's face it, I'm not exactly what one would consider to be a prime catch, now am I? I was well aware of that fact before we left and nothing that has happened since we arrived here has changed that."

"Well the Professor does seem rather taken with you. How do you feel about him?"

"I like him fine. But as for him being a prospective mate, I'm not sure. You think he's taken with me?"

"Oh yes. Not that I have a wealth of experience in these matters, but I do know a thing or two. And I would say that the Professor is smitten with you!"

"Please stop calling him Professor. He really dislikes that name. He puts up with it from the men he works with because they all go by nicknames."

"So what should I call him?"

"Call him by his proper name, Theodore."

Chloe thought to herself, "Hmm, if I were him I think I would prefer to be called Professor."

"Okay I shall call him Theodore if you wish."

"It's not what I wish that matters, it is, in fact, his name!"

"Okay, and I shall apologize to him the very next time I should happen to see him. Which, as past experience has shown us, should be this evening."

"What? This evening? Why do you think we will be seeing him this evening? Do you know something I don't?"

"I can read a calendar. He comes by every third day. Regular, like clockwork. You can count on it."

"I hadn't noticed. How curious. You know I think I shall go and bathe if you don't need me for anything."

Chloe smiled, "No I don't need you. You run off and bathe. Mind that you don't heat the water too much. It's plenty hot from the sun."

Andrea slowly opened her eyes and found herself in a tent. It took her a moment to understand and remember what happened and when some clarity had returned, she realized she was in a Navajo teepee.

Sitting next to her, cross-legged on the ground, was a very old man with extremely wise eyes. He was staring at her and chanting something in a language she did not understand. As her eyes grew accustomed to the dim light she saw that the teacher was standing next to him.

"Teacher!"

The woman smiled at Andrea and said, "That's right I'm the teacher."

"You speak English. I didn't expect…"

"I speak English, Spanish and a bit of French. My tribe sent me to college. My name is Yellow Bird, but call me Mary. All my friends at college called me Mary."

The old man said something to Mary and she turned and said to Andrea, "He wants to know if you remember what happened."

"Yes I do. I was watching you and you found me. I ran and then fainted."

Mary relayed the message to the old man who smiled and nodded.

"That's good, he says. He was worried that you may have hurt your head, he checked you while you were unconscious but couldn't find any indication that you had done any damage. He just wanted to make sure."

"Is he a doctor? Did the tribe send him to college as well?"

Mary laughed, "No. He's the medicine man – I guess we would call him a doctor. No he was trained by a medicine man before him."

"That's so interesting. I want to be a doctor. Or rather I wanted to be a doctor, but we moved from England so my sister could marry her true love, as she calls him. And that was the end of my medical career. So now I snoop around where I have no business being. I am so sorry about that."

"We didn't mind. We knew you had been watching for some time. But it is so hot today, and the chief was worried about you – a little white girl sitting in the hot sun. He sent me to get you and bring you to our camp so you sit near us – in the shade."

"You knew I was watching?"

"Yes, probably from the first day you squatted behind that tumbleweed. They don't make very good hiding places you know. You would have been more concealed behind a cactus."

Andrea blushed, "So why didn't you chase me away?"

"You weren't hurting anyone or anything. And the children loved it - it was like an audience. And children love to perform for an audience, as you may know."

"I don't have a lot of experience with children. I'm the youngest of three girls. I guess I did the performing, come to think of it."

The medicine man spoke to Mary and she went to the fire and brought back a bowl of what appeared to be red tea. She handed it to Andrea and said, "He says for you to drink this. It will help get your strength back."

Andrea was leery but obeyed. She had a sip. It tasted like berries, berries of a sort she had never tasted. She took a few more sips.

"What is that? I think I like it!"

"It's made from roots, berries and leaves. It is very good for you and quite refreshing. You'll see! But you have to be careful, if you drink too much it will make you sick. You have to know how much is safe to drink in order for it to do any good. I tried making it myself when I was a little girl. My stomach hurt for two days."

Andrea lifted the bowl to her mouth to have another small sip and the medicine man uttered something and held up his hand to indicate that she should stop.

Mary said, "You've had enough for now."

He took the bowl from her and motioned for her to stand and take a few steps.

At first she was a little dizzy but the feeling passed quickly and she said to him, "Good as new. Thank you and sorry for causing so much trouble."

Mary translated and he smiled, shook his head and said something.

"He says it was no trouble but that you should not sit in the sun for too long from now on."

"I won't. I've learned my lesson. And I won't be snooping around here anymore."

"No, don't stop. I would like you to come and join our class, if you want. The children will love it and it will give you a chance to get to know us."

"My sister's husband said I shouldn't get too close, he says that the Navajo like to be left alone."

"Usually. Our experiences with the white man have not been good ones I'm afraid. But I think you and I can become good friends. And if you want you can talk to the medicine man and learn a little more about his medicine."

"I would love that. Is it okay if I tell my sisters and Bill? Bill is my sister Chloe's husband."

"Oh we know Bill, very nice man. Keeps to himself. And yes, you should tell them. They should know where you are. This isn't a city, if something should happen while you are wandering around out here it would take a very long time to find you. Make sure people know where you plan to be."

"You sound like Chloe."

"Chloe sounds wise! Okay, are you ready?"

"Ready for what?"

"The chief would like to meet you and I'm sure the children would like to say hello. Some of them have learned a bit of English and would like to try it out on a native speaker."

"Sounds delightful. But am I dressed properly? I

mean, I am meeting a chief after all."

Mary chuckled, "He's a chief, not royalty! What you're wearing is fine."

The teacher led her out of the teepee and on to meet the chief. The people gathered at the entrance to the tent, stared at her and watched every movement.

"You'll have to forgive them, most have seen white men before, but it is seldom we get to see a woman. And never this close. Also, I'm certain no one has seen blonde hair before - at least not as blonde as you."

After she had met the chief and listened to his lecture on the dangers of running around in the hot sun without a companion, Andrea was taken to meet the children and their mothers.

Initially there was a bit of a communication problem but motioning, hand gestures, facial expression and sound effects overcame that little issue rather quickly. And Mary's translation skills helped a great deal. The children could not keep their hands off Andrea's long yellow hair. They were totally fascinated with it and her -- with the exception of one toddler. He took one look at Andrea and started howling in terror, tears streaming down his cheeks.

The sun was on its daily downward journey when Andrea finally said goodbye and made her way back to the house, accompanied by Mary and two young men who seemed quite enchanted by the white woman with the yellow hair.

She entered the house and had no sooner sat down on a kitchen chair when Chloe shouted, "Andrea, there you are! We have to leave the house for the evening. You and I are having dinner in town. Bill is on the trail and won't be back for a couple of days."

"So why does that mean we have to leave? I don't understand. And what about Margaret? Or has she decided to stop eating?"

"Margaret is having a gentleman caller this evening!"

"There is nothing strange about that. There are gentleman callers here just about every night."

"Tonight is different, there is to be but one caller this evening. And this gentleman is coming with the express purpose of spending time and dining with our Miss Margaret!"

Margaret was in a dither. She was very much out of her element. She had boyfriends in London and had been out on dates before, but this was different. Whereas the men in London had been basically friends, no real romantic attraction – she was very much attracted to Theodore. They had so much in common and he was rather cute, which certainly helped. The spectacles however, did little to enhance his looks. Margaret disliked spectacles, they did not seem natural – metal and glass strapped to your face, it just wasn't right.

"I wonder if he really needs them," she had asked Chloe that afternoon. Chloe had replied that she was certain he wouldn't have chosen to wear them otherwise. Margaret put it out of her mind.

Now, as she rushed around tidying the house, and putting the finishing touches on dinner, something struck her. What happens if it turns out he doesn't feel about me as I feel for him? This could be awkward.

She decided that rather than throw herself at him, she would be reserved - at least until she could ferret out his feelings towards her. That would be best. No sense leaving herself open to humiliation and hurt. Well, alright she would be hurt whether or not she showed him her feelings, but at least it wouldn't be out there in the open for all to see.

She did not want to be pitied. She had known girls who had thrown themselves at men only to be rejected. Everyone pitied them, which just added to the humiliation and misery.

One such acquaintance, having been publicly rejected, had actually run away and joined a convent. She was never heard from again. The funny thing was – the man doing the rejecting was heartbroken. It turned out that the only reason he had shunned her advances was that he did not want to seem too eager. In truth, she was the only woman for him. The last Margaret had heard, he was still single and drinking himself to death in London's east end.

"People! No wonder I prefer the company of books," Margaret said aloud as she set the table.

She had just finished placing the last utensil on the table when there was a timid little knock at the door.

While Margaret was preparing to entertain Theodore, her two sisters were being seated at a table in the hotel dining room. Santa Fe had only two restaurants, the one in the hotel and one attached to the saloon. They had wandered by the saloon just as a cowboy, one they recognized as a man who had been by their house on numerous occasions, was being unceremoniously tossed out on his face.

He appeared to be very drunk. After helping him to his feet and sending him on his way, they decided the hotel dining room would probably be more suited to a quiet dinner.

It was anything but a quiet meal as Andrea started to tell Chloe about her Navajo adventure that day. She had been reluctant to say anything for fear of a reprimand over approaching their neighbors – especially after she had been explicitly warned to stay away from them. Not that Chloe had really expected her to heed the caution.

She listened slack jawed as Andrea unraveled the tale of the teacher, the medicine man and the chief. She had grown up reading tales of the Wild West and was relieved that the Indians had left her hair intact and told Andrea so.

"That is so… I don't know what to call it," Andrea replied.

"I'm sorry but I worry about you. You are my responsibility, you know. Your safety is all mine for at least another year or, God willing, until you get married. You're not going back there are you? Oh, you are, aren't you? You're planning on going back."

"Of course I am. It is fascinating. And I think I just may learn a little about medicine. The medicine man said I could watch him and learn. And Mary said I would be more than welcome to help her with the children. At least I'll be doing something. It's better than sitting around the house entertaining cowboys. And much better than waiting for someone to marry me."

"You know, I am going to have to discuss this with Bill. I don't know how happy he is going to be."

"I know you are trying to be a mother to me. But I am a woman. And you don't have to baby me. And Bill is my brother-in-law, not my father. He has no right to say what I can and cannot do."

"I understand how you feel. But you are living in Bill's house and the Navajo are his neighbors. I would just feel better if we told him about it and see how he feels. I'm sure once he knows how strongly you feel about this, he'll gladly give you his blessing. It's just a little show of respect. Okay?"

"Okay, but only as a sign of respect. I am not looking for his permission. Is that okay?"

"Yes, of course it is. By the way, were there any good looking men there?"

Back at the house, dinner was finished and the couple decided to go for a stroll under the stars.

Margaret had never seen a sky as brilliant as that spread out above the New Mexico countryside. It was as if the cosmos was putting on a display just for them, and she said so.

Theodore smiled, "There's a bit of the poet in you isn't there. We've never talked about poetry. Do you read poetry?"

"Yes I do. It took a long time for me to get interested in it though. I think that is the result of being forced to study it in school. I didn't mind reading it, but I hated being told what it meant or what it was showing us. I think poetry is personal to the reader, and what one person understands it to be saying is not necessarily what another might think.

Don't you agree?"

"Whole heartedly. I liked poetry when I was a boy, but it wasn't really a boy thing to be doing – reading poetry. I did not tell a soul. Life would have been unbearable. I grew up in Texas, boys didn't read poetry unless they were forced to. And you sure didn't admit that you actually enjoyed it."

"I understand. That's a bit like Andrea. She's been engrossed in science since she could read. Not very girl like, at least not in England. Everyone thought she was just a foolish little girl and she would outgrow it. She hasn't. If anything, she seems to be growing more interested. Did you know that she wanted to be a doctor? A woman doctor, have you ever heard of such a thing?"

"No I haven't. All the doctors out here are men, and the nurses are women. Would she like to be a nurse? I know the doctor in Santa Fe is looking for someone to train. His nurses keep getting married and leaving to have babies. Maybe they be should be training men to be nurses."

Margaret laughed, "Male nurses! I think that is less likely than female doctors. You've got quite the imagination you do."

They decided that they had walked enough and turned to return to the house and the apple pie that Margaret had made for dessert. As they turned, Theodore reached out and gave her a hug, kissing her tenderly on her cheek. Her eyes widened and she embraced him, returning the kiss, but hers was full on the mouth. It was now quite clear how they felt about each other. There was to be no humiliation, no hurt and no pity.

Within a week Theodore became a fixture at the Butler household and Bill was glad of it. Keeping three women entertained was tiring business and having grown up in an all male household, it was something he had little knowledge of.

Margaret and Theodore entertained themselves, they could usually be found outside, sitting under a tree discussing some book or another. It was clear for all to see that they were in love.

Bill had no problem with his sister-in-law's choice of a man, he had always found the Texan to be a good friend, and by all indications, he would make a good husband. So he was not at all surprised when Theodore came to him ate one afternoon and asked for Margaret's hand in marriage.

He promptly agreed but inquired, "Have you asked her yet? It's one thing to get my approval, and I am very flattered that you would ask me, but have you asked Margaret? And it might be a good idea to ask Chloe."

"Well I wanted some sort of a go ahead from you first. If you objected I was not going to ask, but now… well, I am going to ask her tonight. We're going to town for dinner and I plan to ask her then. Only after she says yes will I ask Chloe."

"I've seen the way she looks at you. And I may be telling tales out of school, but when you aren't around you're all she talks about. I have a pretty good hunch what her answer is going to be. So where are you planning on living? You can't move her into the bunkhouse. And I don't think she'd appreciate sleeping under the stars."

"I want to start building a house for us. Just

something small for now. But I am going to wait until she says yes. Can I count on you for some help building it? It shouldn't take much time. I'll just need some help getting the walls up. I can handle the rest myself."

"Of course I'll help. I was scared you were going to say you were moving in here. That would be mite crowded. If I would have known what was going to happen, I would have made this place bigger," Bill laughed, "And we still have to get Andrea married off."

"Oh Andrea. I almost forgot. I was at the doc's today for a sore back and I told him about her interest in medicine. He said he would love to meet her, he could use her as a nurse. It would only be part time. Mornings mostly. Afternoons he's usually making house calls or at the hospital. He really needs some help."

"I can ask her, but she is spending most of her time with the Navajo. From what it sounds like, she has an admirer there. I don't know how serious it is, but she comes home awfully happy. Anyway, I will ask, it doesn't hurt to ask. Although I have to admit she does scare me some. I don't like to upset her, she's a very strong woman. Puts me in mind of my grandmother, God rest her soul.

"That was one tough woman. She built the house my father grew up in. And she fought Indians. In those days, fighting between the cattlemen and Indians was very common. So yeah, I am terrified of Andrea. But I will ask her if she would be interested in nursing. But not today. Today you and Margaret have all the attention. This is your night."

"I really appreciate this. Okay it's time to take her

to town for dinner. Wish me luck!"

"You don't need it. She's madly in love with you."

That night, instead of going to bed immediately after dinner, as was his habit when he had to be up 'roping and riding' early in the morning, Bill sat up with Chloe and Andrea waiting for Margaret and Theodore to return from town. He had not said a word about Theodore's plans for the evening. Time dragged but finally they heard the clicking of the carriage wheels as the couple pulled up in front of the house.

Theodore was beaming, Margaret was blushing as she said, "We have some news…"

One down, Bill thought to himself as he winked at Chloe.

That night the happy group celebrated until the wee small hours of the morning.

When Bill got up the next day he was surprised to find a sullen Andrea having coffee in the kitchen.

"Good morning! You're up early today, aren't you?"

"Yes, it's going to be a long day I'm afraid. Several of the Navajo children are quite ill and the medicine man needs help. I don't know how much help I can be, but I guess it's better than nothing. Those poor kids."

"What's wrong with them?"

"He isn't sure, but I think it's the pox. I've seen small children afflicted with it in London and this sure looks just like it."

"What can you do? Can it be cured?"

"No I don't think so. I think the best we can do is just keep them as comfortable as possible until it runs its course. And pray of course. They are just burning up. We keep putting cold compresses on them and giving them baths in cold water. It seems to help. And of course, they scratch at the sores until they bleed. The itching drives them crazy. We can't let them scratch. There is too great a risk of infection. And once infection sets in there is not a lot we can do."

"I guess this is a bad time to ask you if you'd be interested in helping the doctor in town. He really needs some help."

"I probably would love that, but until this passes I can't even think about it, I'm sorry. I would love to help, you must know that. But these children…"

"No I understand. It's okay. Do you want me to get the doc to come out there?"

"I don't think anyone there would appreciate that, but I will talk to Mary and see what she thinks. If it gets much worse we may have to do that. But let's keep it as a last resort. Thank you for your concern. I was going to say something last night, but what with Margaret's news I didn't think it appropriate. Besides it wouldn't have helped anything."

"You're right. It wouldn't. Can I at least give you a ride out to the camp."

"Oh I would appreciate that, thank you so much. I was just leaving the girls a note, I may stay out there tonight if they need me. That's okay, isn't it?"

"Of course it is. You certainly don't need my permission. And if there is anything we can do to help out you just tell us, okay? Anything, anything at all."

"I will, but as I said, there is not a whole lot that

can be done right now. But you could say a prayer if you're that way inclined."

"Do the Navajo believe in God?"

"The Great Spirit. Yes they do. He's called the Great Spirit but it's the same concept."

"I see. Okay let's get you out there. Ready to go?"

When they arrived at the Navajo encampment, Mary was trying her best to console a very upset woman, her only child had been stricken during the night.

"I am glad you came today, it's going to be busy. Another three children fell sick during the night. I haven't had any sleep. And Bill, it's nice to see you again. It's been a long time. Have you come to help?"

"Hi Mary. No I'm afraid I've got work to do. But I can come back after I'm done and lend a hand if you need."

"That would be so kind of you. We would really appreciate it. Our men say that the sickness is the work of an evil spirit. They want the children out of the camp to move the evil away from the rest of us. But I think they just don't like seeing or being around sick children. It's too heart breaking. Especially when we can't do anything but wait it out."

Bill replied, "If you want, I can get the doctor. I'm sure he'd come out."

"I suspect that he may have his hands full with sick children in town. I doubt if he will have time to come out here. This will spread though the valley, you can count on it."

"Well if there is anything I can do, you tell Andrea and I'll be out."

Andrea had gone straight to a family she had been with the day before. The young mother was caring for three children in various stages of the illness and Andrea was anxious to see if there had been any improvement over night. She was familiar with pox and had read a little on it the night before. Margaret had a good collection of medical books that she had brought from London, thinking that they would be something they could read on the ship.

The oldest of the three sick children appeared to be much better but the baby seemed to be having a hard time. She got to work sponging down the poor infant.

The medicine man was making his rounds, checking on the children and administering a concoction, which seemed to help bring the fever down. All of the mothers were exhausted and in need of some rest. Andrea spent the morning going from family to family, offering to take care of the children giving the mothers the opportunity to get some rest. The mothers refused to leave.

And that is how the rest of Andrea's day went. Finally, as evening was falling and the men were returning to camp, she was allowed to care for the sick as the mothers attended to the men.

As she and Mary were sitting in a tent with two little girls, attempting to force feed them some of the medicine prescribed by the medicine man, a man entered. It was the young fellow who had been so taken with her. He attempted to strike up a conversation with her, using Mary as a translator.

Andrea discovered that he was a year older than she was and was to be trained by the medicine man. He would become the tribe's medicine man in due course. Andrea related how she had wanted to become a doctor, but ended up in America.

"Well you can become a medicine woman," the young man said in reply.

"Is there such a thing? I thought that was a man's job."

"Yes it is, but as you can see our medicine man has more work than he can handle. The Navajo population has grown the last few years and there are not a lot of medicine men."

"That is something I will have to think about. Now, do you mean I could work here?"

"The chief would have to approve it, but I am sure our medicine man would appreciate the help. Especially at times like this. By the way, did you know you have a Navajo name?"

"What? I have a name? What do the people call me?"

"Day Woman. Because you used to watch us every day. I think it's a nice name, don't you?"

"I do. I like it. Day Woman," Andrea repeated the name about a dozen times as if she were trying on a new dress. She smiled and the young man laughed. Mary stood next to Andrea and chuckled.

"Well since you have given me my Navajo name, I'm going to give you a suitable English name. I think I shall call you Luke. That is a good name for a medicine man."

"Luke. I like it. Luke." And following Andrea's lead, he repeated the name several times.

The three of them burst out laughing, waking the sleeping patients. The noise was deafening and the trio turned their attention to the children.

Andrea was in her element; if she couldn't be a doctor she would become a medicine woman. She loved the idea and she loved her new name, she could not wait to get home and tell her sisters. And of course she would have to tell them about Luke.

Margaret's wedding date was set and the preparations had been made. The couple had decided not to waste any time and were to be married the week following their announcement. Theodore and Bill had slapped together a livable house in a matter of two days. The house would still need some finishing but that could be done later. Theodore had already moved in and declared that it 'much better than the bunkhouse'.

Bill was starting to see a glimpse of the day when he and his bride would have some privacy and be able to get on with a proper marriage. But there was still the matter of Andrea, or Day Woman -- as she insisted they call her. At first Chloe thought this was just another of her flights of fancy, this whole medicine woman affair, but it was clear that she had decided that this was to be her path.

Chloe knew, from long experience, that once her youngest sister had set her mind on something there was little anyone could do to change it. She decided that rather than fight her, she would be supportive. Her growing fondness for Luke was another matter. It was obvious that he had set his cap for her, and Chloe could not help but wonder how the matter was being dealt with among the Navajo elders.

Bill advised her to let it go, saying, "The more you fight it, the more she is going to pursue it. If there is something there, you won't be able to stop it. If there isn't, it will die a natural death."

"But I am responsible for her. I don't want her making a mistake that is going to cause her heartache."

She tried to imagine what their parents would have said, had they lived. Not that Andrea listened to them all that well. She guessed that they too would have had serious misgivings about a mixed marriage. They had been brought up in times that dictated against mixed marriages of any shape, size or form - starting with race and ending with religion.

"You're probably right. And if she does up and marry Luke, we will have our house to ourselves and maybe even start our own family. Right?"

But that day, when Andrea arrived at the camp, she could feel something was not right. The children were well on their way to recovery, and she planned on spending the day taking care of the few who were still running fevers and scratching at their sores. But the people seemed to be going out of their way to avoid her. The feeling was palpable.

She finally asked Mary, "Why is everybody shunning me this morning?"

"It's your friend Luke. I guess he went to talk to the chief about you and him. He seems to have it in his head that you and he should get married. And I'm afraid that a marriage of that sort is not looked upon favorably here. The same as in your community, I'm sure."

"My sister has been giving me some grief over it. I think it is nobody's business but our own, I wish people would just mind their own business. Is there any way you can talk to the chief? Or do you think that this is wrong?"

"No I think that any kind of love is good. Even love between people of different races. There is enough hate in this world. But it is not what I think that matters here. I can talk to the chief for you. And I should talk to the medicine man as well. He is counting on Luke to take over when he is no longer able to perform his duties. What about your family? Do they know about this?"

"My sister Margaret is more concerned with her own marriage. But even so, she doesn't care; she just wants me to be happy. Bill just floats along, he doesn't like to see anyone unhappy, and the sooner I'm out of his house the sooner he can get down to the business of starting a family. They haven't been alone – ever.

"There has always been someone around, even on their wedding night. But as for Chloe, well that's where the problem comes in. She really wants me to be happy but she just doesn't trust my judgment. As far as she is concerned I'm still just a little girl."

"I'm afraid there is not much I can do for you as far as your family goes, I wish there were. But I will talk to the chief and medicine man today. Don't worry about how the people are acting, once the chief gives his approval, their attitudes will change. That much I can promise you."

Andrea went about her work that morning trying to avoid contact with the Navajo adults. The children had no problem with her, and those who had recovered enough were eager to engage her in play. She spent the morning with the children and then decided that there was no real need for her to spend the entire day. Everything was under control and she wanted to get away from the eyes that were staring right through her. She would go home and wait for the results of Mary's meeting with the chief.

"What are you doing home so early," Chloe demanded as she returned to the house.

Andrea explained the situation at the camp, and broke into tears, sobbing as she said, "And to make matters worse, you are against us too!"

Chloe stared at her for a minute, thinking about her baby sister's predicament. Then it hit her.

"You love him. You really love him! I don't believe this. I thought you were just being your impetuous self. But you really care for him, don't you?"

Andrea was sobbing much too hard to speak and just nodded.

"Alright then. If you are sure this is what you want, I will support you. I hate to see you this way. Now, what can I do to help? Do you want me to go out there and talk to the chief? And I should meet Luke. I've just seen him a couple of times when he walked you home. I want to get to know him."

Chloe was now in agreement, and in control, and Andrea was glad, but the last thing she wanted - the last thing she needed - was for her sister to confront the Navajo chief. She could be very frightening when she was fighting for a cause about which she felt strongly. And it was not a pretty sight. She did not want her going out there and terrifying the Navajo nation. She would end up starting a war.

"No that's fine. Mary is going to plead our case. She's a lot like you in many ways. I think that's why we get along so well."

"So what do we do now? When is she having her meeting?"

"She didn't say when, she just said sometime today. I think it depends on how busy the chief is. He has to deal with the men first before he concerns himself with women and children."

Chloe frowned, "Some things are exactly the same as they are in England, aren't they?"

"They sure are."

In order to help pass the time, they decided a trip to town was just the thing they needed. Andrea had still not gone to see the doctor, and as her future as a medicine woman seemed somewhat unsure, she decided this would be an opportune time to visit.

Once they found the doctor's office - no easy feat as the doctor's residence doubled as his place of business - they entered quietly. They stood and waited in what passed for the reception area. There was but a single chair and Chloe insisted that Andrea take it.

"You're the one under all this pressure. Sit and rest."

The office was deathly quiet, not a sound to be heard anywhere, and they were just about to leave when Chloe spotted a bell with a rope hanging from it.

"Hmmm, let's try this, shall we. The sign out front said 'The doctor is in', he must be around somewhere."

She reached up and pulled the rope several times setting off a clanging that they were sure could be heard all the way to the Navajo camp. After waiting a couple of minutes she rang it again.

This time, a door opened and voice said, "I'll be right with you. I'm just with a patient right now. I'm sorry – no nurse here. Please have a seat."

"Well, nice sounding voice, he sounds kind," Chloe quipped and then added, "And he needs a nurse."

A very nervous Andrea smiled and said, "There may be some hope for me after all. Unless he was looking for a male nurse."

Chloe laughed and said, "Good! You've still got your sense of humor."

It took fifteen minutes for the doctor to finish up with his patient, a boy of about eight years, clearly suffering from the pox. The boy and his mother listened as the doctor went over his instructions and finished with, "And Mrs. Douglas, remember keep him out of the light. Put him in a dark room. The light is hard on his eyes right now."

The mother thanked him and left.

The doctor watched as they left and then turned to the girls and said, "Now young ladies. My name is Doctor Sinclair. What brings you here today? Which one of you is the patient? Or do you both need to see me?"

The women looked at each other, unsure of who should do the speaking. Finally, Chloe jumped in and explained why they were there.

"Oh there is a God," the doctor exclaimed, "You my girl, are heaven sent. As you can see I have a real need for a nurse."

Andrea finally spoke up, "I have to tell you - I have no training."

"Yes, but you have practical experience.

Sometimes that's worth more than all the training in the world. Anything you need to know while on the job, I can teach you."

"Now how would you know I have experience?" Andrea was puzzled; did the events of the past couple of weeks show in her face in a way she was unaware of?

The doctor smiled, "I have been out to see the Navajo on several occasions since this pox outbreak, and they have told me about an English lady who has been helping them. You are the only English women around, other than our librarian and I was sure she wasn't spending her days out there."

"You've been out to see them? Why haven't I seen you there?"

"I go out there late at night, after my duties here are taken care of. And I wouldn't really like it to get out that I am helping them. It upsets some of the folks around here. They feel that my only duty should be to them. They say I have no business treating the Navajo. So rather than waste time arguing with the few ignorant souls who would have the Indians go without medical attention, I go out there under the cover of darkness."

The girls were speechless.

"So when can you start," he smiled and added, "I don't know if you have heard but we are in the middle of a pox outbreak. And I can use the help."

"I can start right now if you want!"

"You have made an old doctor very happy. Okay, our first patient is here."

They looked around, not a soul was to be seen.

"Is there a patient in the examination room?"

"No my dear nurse, your first patient is going to

be your sister."

"Chloe," she turned to look at her sister, "are you okay?"

"As far as I know. I feel fine."

"Ah then you aren't aware," the doctor stated adding, by way of an explanation, "Unless I am sadly mistaken, and in thirty-three years of practicing medicine I have never been wrong in these matters, you are about six weeks pregnant."

"Pregnant?"

"Yes my dear, now let's get you into the examination room and see how it's coming along. Are you coming nurse?"

And in a matter of a morning Andrea became the first nurse in New Mexico to come from England.

Epilogue

About eight months later, Chloe and Bill became the proud parents of a healthy baby boy they named Luke. He would grow up to become one of the first senators from the great state of New Mexico, which finally attained statehood on January 6th, 1912 - becoming the 47th state in the United States of America.

The couple went on to have five more children, for a total of six – five girls and just the one boy. They remained in the same house, but Bill spent a great deal of his spare time constructing additional rooms in order to make room for everyone.

He greatly appreciated the opportunity to be out of the house when all the women were congregated.

He finally gave up cow punching after the birth of their last daughter, and went into the house building business.

Margaret and Theodore married, but sadly were not blessed with children. Theodore continued as a cowboy until an accident damaged his back so severely that he could not ride a horse. His roping and riding days behind him, he opened a livestock supply store in Santa Fe. Margaret became good friends with Madeline the librarian, spending her days helping out.

She eventually started teaching in the school and took over as librarian when Madeline married and left to start her own family. As his first project as a house builder, Bill constructed a house for them, half way between the library and Theodore's place of business.

The Navajo's chief's verdict concerning the matter of Andrea and Luke finally came down after three months of deliberation. He expressly forbade a marriage between the pair. Luke went on to become the tribe's medicine man as Andrea labored happily for Doctor Sinclair for three years.

The old doctor saw something of a gift in Andrea's treatment of patients, and arranged and paid for her to attend Harvard medical school, where she met a young medical student named Matthew Johnson. The two were married the day after graduation. They moved back to New Mexico, settling in Albuquerque. Together, they opened a medical practice, the services of which were made available to people of all races, creeds and colors.

They would have three children, two boys and a girl – John, Silas and Florence. Silas and Florence were her parents' names.

Andrea and Luke are still close fiends and she

visits him when she is in Santa Fe seeing her family. The girls never returned to England.

THE END

Doreen Milstead

Mail Order Bride: Three Sisters & Ships, Trains & Stagecoaches Out West

Synopsis: Mail Order Bride: Three Sisters & Ships, Trains & Stagecoaches Out West - A woman and her two sisters fall on hard times in England when their alcoholic father dies, so they all decide to go out west and seek mail order husbands. Only one has actually corresponded with a rancher but throughout the long journey by ship, train and stagecoach, she wonders if he'll still be there at the end, and also, what will happen to her beloved sisters.

Esther rested on a chair watching her sisters. Their world had crumbled around them in a matter of days. Each one struggled to deal with the shock in their own particular way. Isabella stood beside the window staring out at the pear tree with its delicate flowers dancing on the breeze. She was likely composing a beautiful poem or perhaps planning which colors to use in her next painting. The youngest of the three, she found solace in her art.

Charlotte had collapsed onto the sofa in a storm of tears as soon as the services were over. The middle child, she felt everything strongly and had no qualms about letting them out. At least she waited until they were in the privacy of their home.

The home that was theirs no longer. Esther looked around the tiny cottage with a mixture of relief and sorrow stirring in her chest. It was the only home she had ever known, her haven and refuge from the world. It was also full of shadows and memories that threatened to drag her into the black void of despair.

She could not succumb. Her sisters needed her to be strong. Who else was there but her?

"We must make a plan." Esther pitched her voice above Charlotte's sobs. "The landlord will allow us to remain here, but only until he finds a new tenant." She swallowed back her own grief and continued. With no family, no dowry, and only the small stipend from father's will, our options are limited."

"How can you speak so callously and father not yet cold in his grave?" Charlotte cried out, her face twisted by grief into a caricature of her usual cheery beauty. "Some of us loved him, we need time to grieve."

The harsh words cut Esther's heart until it bled. She clenched her hands into fists, digging her nails into her palms until she found her control.

Tenderhearted Isabella moved from the window, perched beside the weeping girl, and rubbed her hand across Charlotte's shoulders in a soothing circle. "Esther loved father too, dearest. We all miss him, but our sister is right. We need to know what we are going to do next." She waited for the inevitable sobs to subside before she continued. "But perhaps, for tonight, we can just be together and let ourselves mourn. Tomorrow will be soon enough for plans."

Esther acknowledged her sister's silent plea. Charlotte would be of no use until she cried herself out and slept through the night. She reined in her own need to secure the future and nodded.

"Very well. We will meet here tomorrow after breakfast." Esther couldn't make herself leave it at that. "In the meantime, each of you must think of something we can do to exist."

Isabella sent her a weak smile and even Charlotte managed to nod.

Esther stood on shaky knees and made her way out to the garden behind the house. A footpath led to a small stone bench surrounded by her mother's rose garden. As a girl, she remembered sitting there, tending her sleeping sisters as Mother fussed among the fragrant blooms. As lovely as a flower herself, Mother had hummed and laughed with the carefree charm of a girl. Esther's best memories were of those days before illness stole her mother away.

"Oh, Mamma, I just don't know what to do. You told me to care for father and my sisters, but I feel like I have failed. Father is gone and I can think of no way to protect the girls from the future." Esther buried her face in her hands and sobbed as hard as Charlotte ever had. "Mamma, I just need someone to tell me what to do."

Of course, there was no one and eventually the tears subsided. The peace of the garden and the soft fragrance of the early blooming roses became a balm to her heart. She closed her eyes and tried to imagine her mother among the roses, trying to draw some measure of comfort from the garden.

"Esther, are you in there?" Isabella called softly.

"I'm here. Did Charlotte calm down?" Esther

made room on the bench and Isabella settled on the hard seat nestling her head on Esther's shoulder.

"Yes, I got her to drink some tea and go to bed. She's sleeping now." Isabella sighed. "Are things really so bad that we must find a way to make a living? Did Father have nothing saved?"

"Very little and after funeral expenses, there is only enough for a short time." Esther reached over to grasp her sister's hand. "We will have to marry or find employment. Perhaps both."

"How can we marry with no dowry, and even then, who in this town would have us? Father's illness was too well known." Isabella dabbed her eyes with a damp handkerchief. Esther had to press her lips closed to keep from speaking her mind.

Illness indeed. Isabella was the one to sugarcoat the truth. Their father was a drunk. He had hidden it well enough while their mother was alive, but when consumption took her five years ago, Father had lost all interest in life save what he found in the bottle. It was true, however, that no one who knew their father would willingly marry his daughters. So, they would have to find someone they did not know.

"Esther," Isabella broke in on her thoughts. "What about America? I have read in 'The Times' that the American west is so lacking in women, that men are advertising in the east, even in Europe, for women to marry."

"Yes, I have heard that as well." In fact, she had already collected several sheets of prospective ads to share with her sisters on the morrow. "I think it would be a very good thing for us, but we will wait to discuss it until Charlotte is fit to join us."

The next day, they sat before the fire crackling on the hearth and scanned the various requests for matrimony. Some, the women dismissed as impossible for reasons that ranged from poor grammar to obvious disqualifications such as looking for a woman with money. Esther's frustration grew as her sisters turned up their noses at men that were suitable. One was too old; another wanted a woman who would raise his children.

One lived in a big city, another excessively remote. Esther considered her sisters too fussy by half. They did finally narrow their choices down to ten men that were not too old, or poor or illiterate. To those men, each sister wrote a letter stating their age and their fulfillment of requirements.

A few of the men replied, others remained silent, and the winnowing process went on. More letters were sent, and more men rejected until one remained.

One man for three sisters.

Oh dear.

Esther read the letter for the third time. The gentleman in question had responded to each of her letters with his own, each one showing integrity, humor, and character. He had not written to either of her sisters, for which she was secretly glad. For Esther very much liked the sound of his letters and wanted to meet him, perhaps marry him herself. This last letter had included enough money to get her to his ranch, enough money for one person traveling economically.

What was she to do with her younger sisters if she were to find a husband for herself? She couldn't very well desert them and leave them to their own devices.

They would be cast out, penniless, into the street. Neither one had the temperament to be a servant in some rich man's home nor had any other skills to recommend them.

She was about to read the letter again, hoping for some sort of inspiration to help her sisters when a knock sounded through the quiet house. A moment later, Isabella appeared in the doorway.

"Esther, a gentleman is here. He would like to speak to you." Isabella grinned and winked as if the caller was there on a personal matter. Not bloody likely.

Esther chastised herself for the ungracious thought. Tucking her precious letter away, she went to the entryway. An elderly gentleman stood there holding his gloves and top hat. The landlord.

"Mr. Thornton, it is a pleasure to see you. Won't you come in?" Esther pasted a smile on her face and gestured toward the gloomy sitting room.

"Thank you, Miss Westcott, but I cannot stay but a moment." He cleared his throat and clenched the brim of his hat with his hands. "I fear I have some news that makes my business here less than pleasant. You see, I have a new tenant for this house and he would like to take residence immediately."

"Oh," Esther put her hand over her heart, which threatened to stop its beating. "I see. It will take us a bit of time to pack. We have done some, but we thought there would be more time."

"I know I have put you in a terrible position, but times being what they are, I need someone here who will be able to pay the rent."

"We are very grateful that you have let us stay as long as you have. I don't know what we would have done otherwise." Esther smiled a genuine smile this time. He really had been very sweet and even now looked as guilty as if he were casting orphans out into the cold. While it was true the sisters were orphans, they were not children who required someone to look after them.

"There is not great rush, I have told him he must wait until you are packed. Do you have somewhere to go?" the old gentleman asked.

The letter against her heart crackled guiltily. "Yes, I have just today received word from a . . . friend in America asking us to come to him. I was just about to accept the invitation when you arrived." Esther touched the old landlord's hand and leaned forward to kiss his wrinkled cheek. "You have been as kind as an uncle would be and we are forever in your debt."

The old cheeks flushed pink. "You are good girls, regardless of what your father was. Take this for your journey. It isn't much. I wish you and your sisters Godspeed." He pressed a banknote into Esther's hand, then turned and rushed out the door.

When it closed, Esther looked down at the banknote in her hand. A hundred pounds. She sank into a nearby chair. To Mr. Thornton it may not have seemed like much, but to her and her sisters, it was a small fortune. This made all the difference in the world.

It meant she could afford to travel to New Mexico and a new life. It also meant she could now take her sisters with her.

"Who was that?" Charlotte opened the door a basket of cut flowers from the garden on her arm. She set down the fragrant burden and untied the ribbons to her hat. "He left in a terrible hurry."

"That was the landlord. He has a new tenant and we need to prepare to leave." Esther eyed Charlotte nervously, but her sister remained composed.

"Well, we knew it was coming." Charlotte rested her hands on her hips and surveyed the dingy hallway. "To be honest, I am happy to be leaving this place."

"You are?" Esther tried to hide her astonishment, but the smirk on her sister's face told her she failed.

"I know I have been a burden to you and Isabella." Charlotte waved away her sister's protest. "Yes I have. It seemed so awful to leave the only home we have ever known, to have no one in this world to turn to. But I have come to a decision."

"And what is that, if I may ask?" Esther sat up straight, the letter and banknote forgotten.

"I have decided that if we were to stay here, life would continue as it always has, without Father of course." Charlotte ran her fingers across the faded paper on the wall. "I thought that was what I wanted, to stay here and everything stay the same. But since reading all those letters from men, I have come to realize that there is a great, wide world out there and there is no reason I can't have a part in it."

"Was there any one man in particular?" Perhaps if Esther could convince her middle sister to accept one of the men as a possible suitor it would leave just one left to care for.

"No, they were all rather staid and boring. I would much prefer a man of elegance and education, but such a man is unlikely to advertise for a wife in a newspaper." Charlotte shrugged. "I will just have to go find him. I will go tell Isabella the good news of our departure."

Esther stared after her sister. What had just

happened?

A few days later, their trunks were loaded into a wagon and the sisters followed along in a hired carriage. The keys to their little cottage had been handed back to a sad landlord and final hugs and promises to write given to the few friends the sisters could claim. Then they settled back in their seats and prepared to face their future.

"Are you certain we cannot afford a new dress or two for each of us?" Charlotte twitched the skirt of her outdated dress mournfully. "You said Mr. Thornton gave us a hundred pounds, surely that would be enough for at least some dress material."

"I'm sorry to disappoint you, but we will need that money for travel expenses. It is a very long way to New Mexico and we do need to eat and sleep along the way." Esther sighed. "I should like to have new things as well, but it just isn't possible."

"We could always make a new dress or two." Isabella looked from one sister to the other. "Our trunks are full of old dresses that we can use. Many of mothers were made during the time of wide hoop skirts and have meters and meters of cloth. Today's dresses are so much slimmer we may even be able to make two dresses out of each one of hers. It will almost be like she is with us."

"I'm not very good at sewing," Charlotte pouted. "And it will take forever."

"Not so long if we work together. The passage to America will take at least a couple of weeks and that should be enough time for each of us to get at least one new dress." Esther said.

"Charlotte, you iron beautifully. I always end up putting in more wrinkles than I take out. And you can sew straight seams well enough; Mother taught you as well as me." Isabella patted her sister's hand cheerfully. "You'll see, Charlotte, we'll have some lovely dresses by the time we reach America."

Once at the waterfront, Esther left her sisters to settle in their small room while she went to the nearby telegraph office. She had to let him know she was coming and warn him that she was bringing her sisters. She had spent most of the carriage ride to town planning what she would say:

Mr. Caleb Jackson
Santa Fe, New Mexico
Am coming to America. STOP. Bringing my 2 sisters. STOP. Cannot leave them alone. STOP. Will make better plans when we arrive. STOP.
Regards,
Esther Westcott

In awe, she watched the telegraph agent tap his little key and send her message flying through the wires across land and sea. She didn't understand how the machine worked, but the operator assured her that Caleb Jackson would receive her message in a matter of hours rather than the weeks that letters required.

Amazing.

Now, she just had to get herself and her sisters there.

The voyage to America took just under ten days.

Far faster than Esther had expected, although she did learn that other ships had made it in as little as seven days with each shipping line striving to outdo the others in quickness. All very well for them, but not nearly enough time to fashion new dresses for each sister.

Therefore, when they disembarked on the New York pier, Charlotte and Isabella sashayed along in new dresses made from their mother's old gowns. Fortunately, their youngest sister was able to fashion new styles with little or no pattern. She could see a dress once and know exactly how to make it work. The necessary bustles had stymied them for a while, but Isabella soon figured out how to make one from the whalebone from an old hoop skirt.

After a week, closed up in their cabin, working furiously with needle and thread, Esther alone still wore the simpler clothing that they had utilized in their English village. She didn't mind, or not much anyway. She at least had a man waiting for her at the end of the journey. Her sisters were the ones who needed to attract male attention.

She cringed inwardly at the mercenary thought, but it was their current reality. Young women with no husbands, no money, and no prospects had few options for bettering their life. The best and easiest course was to find them husbands. And that was not easy at all.

With that goal in mind, Esther carefully scrutinized the men they met throughout their journey. In the early stages, on both ship and train, she kept watch over her sisters. It would not do for them to become enamored of a gentleman so far removed from their destination. It quickly became apparent that she had little to worry about. The recent civil war had decimated the numbers of men to such an extent, that the survivors had their choice of females.

Money was scarcer than men were, and even the beauty of her sisters, which earned more than one appreciative smile, was not enough to overcome their lack of funds. And in Dodge City, Kansas, their money ran out.

Esther sat on the station platform and checked again.

Nothing. How were they going to continue their journey without money?

"Esther, darling, what's wrong? You look ill." Isabella came to sit beside her and touch a cool hand to her sister's brow.

"I am not ill, but we do have a problem." Esther motioned for Charlotte to sit beside her as well. "We are out of money. I was just about to purchase tickets for the last leg of the trip and my purse is empty. We have nothing to eat with much less travel with. I have been so careful, I don't know what happened."

"Perhaps you dropped it or put it in your carpetbag instead." Isabella reached for the faded bag at her sister's feet.

"No, I already checked. I'm afraid it was stolen." Esther forced the words through her lips.

Charlotte stiffened beside her and when Esther looked over, a pink flush covered her sister's cheeks.

"Charlotte, do you know something about this?" Esther bit back a sigh when she saw Charlotte's blush deepen. "Charlotte . . . "

"What, why are you looking at me? I didn't steal it." Charlotte fidgeted and looked across the bustling platform. The train they were supposed to be on, the one that already held their trunks blew its whistle and began to move. Without them.

"Margret Charlotte, where is our money. What have you done with it?" Esther twisted her fingers together to keep from pulling at her hair. She knew that her sister tended to be irresponsible and capricious, but she would never have expected stealing.

"I didn't steal it." Charlotte pouted, but Esther continued to stare. "If you must know, I invested it. And I didn't take all of it. There was some left."

"Yes and I used that to pay our bill at the hotel this morning." Esther took a deep breath. "What do you mean you invested it?"

"He promised that he would pay it back this morning. I tried my best to get it back before you noticed it was gone." Charlotte's chin quivered, but Esther was unmoved.

"He who?"

"Why, it was the gentleman who introduced himself at our table last night, Mr. Adam Sheridan." Charlotte offered a hesitant smile.

"When did you give it to him, certainly not at dinner?" A light was beginning to dawn. Surely, her sister was not so foolish as to give their limited funds to a gambler.

"Oh, no. It was later when you went to the dry goods store for new needles." Charlotte's eyes brightened, glad to be able to provide an explanation. "I was waiting outside and he came out from a door further down the boardwalk. He stopped beside me and we spoke for a moment or two. He was very pleasant and inquired after our destination."

Esther closed her eyes and prayed for patience. "But what about our money?"

"Well, I told him of father's death and you going west to marry a cowboy." Charlotte paused and lowered her eyes bashfully. "He said he was glad that it was you who were going to marry, because it meant there was a chance my heart was still unclaimed."

When her sisters made no response, she continued. "He told me, in confidence you understand, that he was going to Santa Fe himself to run a hotel. He is just in Dodge to raise funds. I went to our room and got a few dollars to invest. It seemed like a good idea to have an interest in the town we are going to be living in, don't you think?"

"Charlotte, dearest, Mr. Sheridan is very likely a confidence man. They make a living tricking people out of their hard earned money and running away with it." Esther felt her anger dissipate. She could not possibly expect her naïve sister to know a swindler from an honest man. It didn't solve the problem of traveling on, but at least she knew what they were dealing with.

"But he was so handsome and agreeable I don't see how he could be dishonest." Charlotte set her lips firmly.

"He wouldn't be able to swindle as many people if he was ugly or nasty would he?" Esther let the subject drop. "We still have a few pieces of Mother's jewelry, perhaps we can sell it."

"Oh no, not mother's jewelry, Esther. Surely there is something else we can do." Isabella's big blue eyes welled up with tears.

"If you can think of something, I would love to hear it. I'm all out of ideas." Esther dug into her carpetbag for the small velvet pouch nestled in with her spare under garments. Fortunately, they had kept the smaller bags with them for easier access while on the train. With any luck, they would meet up with their trunks in Santa Fe in a few days. Her vision misted as he felt the hard shapes within the soft bag. It was the last of their inheritance from Mother.

"There you are Charlotte . . . I mean Miss Westcott. I was afraid you had left on the train. Then I would have had a hard time catching you."

Esther looked up to see a handsome young man tipping his hat to all three sisters although his gaze remained firmly fixed on Charlotte's pink face. The troublesome Mr. Adam Sheridan. She slid the small bag of jewelry back into its hiding place and stood facing him. "Mr. Sheridan, unless you are here to return our money, I will kindly ask you to leave.

The man at least had the decency to blush. "But I do have your money, or at least most of it. That is what I came to tell Charlotte . . . Miss Westcott. I was quite successful last night and I have enough money after all. I came to return your gracious gift." He held out a thin bundle of bills toward Charlotte who gave them to Esther. There was more than she had expected.

"You said 'most of it', I believe." Esther folded her arms and glared at the young man. Charlotte was right in that he didn't look like a confidence man, but then that was the whole point wasn't it. If she didn't know better, she would say that Mr. Sheridan was just another young man full of more dreams than anything practical.

"You are right. I have enough to buy the hotel, but not enough to get me there. I used some of your money to purchase a ticket on the stage. The Overland Stage isn't as fast or convenient as the train, but it is much cheaper."

Esther raised an eyebrow. "How much cheaper?"

He named a price that surprised her. It would get them there with a bit of change to spare. Of course, it didn't include meals, but if they were careful, it could work. "Mr. Sheridan, would you be so kind as to purchase stagecoach tickets for us as well. It seems we will be traveling together for a while longer."

The young man's grin nearly split his face and he removed his hat with a flourish, "nothing would delight me more." Then he took the money from her hand and ran toward a distant building.

"Are we really riding in the stage?" Isabella clapped her hand with excitement. "It will be so exciting. I read about them you know, flying along over the prairie behind the thundering team of horses, held up by bandits and pursued by howling Indians. Oh, sisters I feel this will be the best part of the whole trip."

"Forgive me if I Charlotte our trip is somewhat less eventful than that." Esther said. Neither of her sisters heard her, they were already walking toward the hotel with their heads bent together, one blond one brown. She had to remind herself that they were still rather young; Isabella was not yet twenty and they had both filled their minds with the nonsense printed in dime novels. She supposed it was natural that they think of this journey as an adventure.

At least one sister was sensible enough to think of matters that are more practical. Esther headed to the dried goods store to find cheap and easily carried foods that would sustain them when they could not afford to eat. Then she would send a telegram that would explain their delayed arrival.

Purchases stowed securely in her satchel, Esther walked into the telegraph office to compose her message.

> Mr. Caleb Jackson
> Santa Fe, New Mexico
> Running short of funds. STOP. Left the train to finish our journey by stagecoach. STOP. Am well and tired but in good spirits. STOP. Anxious to see you soon. STOP.
> Warmly,
> Esther Westcott

When she handed it to the agent, he read through it and nodded, then glanced again at her signature at the bottom.

"Pardon me, Miss. Is this you, Miss Esther Westcott?" The man peered at her over wire-framed glasses.

"Yes, that is me. Why do you ask?" She couldn't think of any reason that someone would have to question her identity.

"Well we got a letter in a day or two ago with a note to hold it just in case a young woman of your name came in." The agent reached below the counter and produced an envelope. It did indeed have her name on it in familiar handwriting. She took it to a quiet corner and carefully unfolded the single sheet.

> My Dear Miss Westcott, It began.

I received your telegram and felt the need to write to you. I know you will be traveling and will be uncertain of your whereabouts at any given time so I am writing several notes to be waiting for you along the way. My hope is that you will stop into one of the offices at some point in your journey.

If you are reading this letter, it means that you have arrived in Dodge and more than half your journey is complete. If no one else has said it yet, welcome to America.

I know that this country is not what you are used to and can seem harsh and unpleasant to some. But I know that you are the kind of woman that can see the beauty beneath the barrenness. I think that perhaps you are, judging by your letters. You see the good in people while still acknowledging their shortcomings. Do you know how rare that is?

You wrote of your father with gentleness, although I doubt he was an easy man to live with. You write of your sisters with such deep affection and exasperation that I cannot wait to meet them. And so saying, I come to the purpose of this letter.

I am glad you are bringing your sisters along. Of course, you should not have left them on their own. You say they are quite young and naïve. I know that the three of you answered advertisements for mail order brides. I myself received a letter from each of you. Yours was the only one to touch my heart. Since you are bringing them here, I can only assume that their searching did not bear fruit.

So bring them here, dearest Esther, if I may be so bold has to call you that; bring them to my ranch and we will be a family together. Let them grow and mature a little and perhaps they will eventually find a man who touches their hearts as you have touched mine. Even if they do not, they will be welcome here for as long as they wish.

I do not have much and my home is small, but somehow we will manage. What is mine is yours.

Earnestly yours,
Caleb Jackson

Esther let the paper flutter to her lap. She blinked furiously to hold back the tears. To have someone so warm and welcoming offer to share her burden seemed like a miracle. How had she been so fortunate as to gain the affection of one so perfect?

At length she gathered up her letter and joined her sisters and Mr. Sheridan at the stagecoach terminal. Four mismatched horses shifted around nervously. They had rough coats and small compared to the English thoroughbreds that she had known, but they looked sturdy and anxious to run. She prayed they would run far and fast.

The Concord stage showed evidence of bright paint under a thick coating of reddish dust. She handed her carpetbag to the driver who piled with the other luggage strapped to the top. Mr. Sheridan handed her into the coach followed by Isabella and Charlotte then he climbed in after them. With just the four of them, there would have been plenty of room to relax, but two more people climbed in.

The first was a middle-aged gentleman wearing a black broadcloth suit and mutton chop whiskers. A gold watch chain looped across his ample belly and twinkled in the light. He clutched a leather satchel on his lap and refused to allow the driver to put it in the boot.

"Very important papers, you know. Mustn't let them out of my sight." The whiskered man tipped his hat revealing a balding pate, then shifted his grip back to the satchel, his knuckles turning white.

The other gentleman to climb in was a soldier dressed in the bold blue and yellow of the union army. He nodded to the other passengers and took the last seat beside the window where he stared out to the street with a blank gaze.

Just as the driver had folded up the step and closed the door, another man holding a saddle slung across his back sauntered up.

"Any room left?" He peered in the window opposite the soldier and grinned cheekily. "Nope, I would say ye got a full house today. You Ok with me ridin' on top? Boss says to get back to the Bar S quick 's I can."

"Sure thing, son. There's been tales of the Comanche raidin' off the reservation again, so every gun we can claim is that much more security for the rest of us." The driver jerked a thumb toward the top. "Ye c'n stow your saddle up there."

"Them Commanches are the reason I'm headed back. We only left a few hands back at the ranch to keep an eye on things. Trouble is, their all green as a Tennessee valley, likely never saw a wild Indian in the whole of their lives" The young cowboy continued his friendly chatter as he slung the heavy saddle to the top of the stage as though is weighed nothing.

"Me, I rode with the Indians now and again when I was a youngster. Good folks, but there ain't no way for the young bucks to earn the affection of the maidens when they're stuck on the reservation. The way to an Indian girl's heart ain't through flowers and tender words like our white girls." The cowboy glanced in the window and winked at the sisters who all stared at him with wide eyes. "No sir, the way to an Indian maid's heart is lots of horses and scalps."

Esther heard Isabella's gasp at the words. She had trouble understanding it as well, who could find violence and thievery to be positive attributes? The cowboy must have heard the gasp as well. He leaned a sun-browned arm on the window and peered in. His eyes met Isabella's and he winked again, undaunted by her upturned, stubborn chin.

"Now me, if I wanted to win a girl, I'd tell her that she was prettier than a mountain sunrise with her hair all golden with bits of stardust and moonbeams sprinkled in. I'd say how her eyes were as deep and pretty a blue as the summer sky just after a rainstorm with everything washed new and clean. I'd tell her how to wake beside her of a morning would make me the richest man on earth, though I ain't got two plugged nickels to rub together."

The driver guffawed and slapped his knee before he climbed up into his seat. Several other onlookers chuckled as well. Esther eyed Isabella's red face with interest.

"Well, boy, you might need more than some pretty words to win those ladies over." The driver's words drifted down from the box above the coach. "Most ladies I know are looking for something more than a drifter to settle down with."

The cowboy's cheeky grin faded for a moment or two, and then it was back as he tipped his hat one more time and climbed up to his perch at the top of the coach. "You think what you like Charlie, the right girl will come along who will know that love is more important than money."

Still laughing, the driver cracked his whip and the horses lurched into a run throwing Esther and her sisters against the thin cushions.

"Do you really think there will be Indians?" Charlotte pitched her voice over the thunder of running hooves and the rattling of the stage.

Scrunched between the other men, Mr. Sheridan shrugged. "It is always a possibility. The tribes out here are not as settled as those further east. Often they will stay on the reservation through the winter months then go raiding when the weather warms. If your party is strong enough, they will generally leave you alone."

"And is our party strong enough, do you think?" Esther asked. She had not given much thought to Indian attacks when she made the decision to bring her sisters out here. She wondered if she had sentenced them all to death.

"We are pretty well armed. Both the driver and the shotgun rider will be armed with a Winchester repeating rifle or a shotgun, possibly both. Our cheeky cowboy rider will undoubtedly have a rifle of some sort as well as at least one side arm. They are both necessary to anyone who rides the range." Mr. Sheridan nodded toward the soldier who appeared to doze with his head pillowed by his hat against the wall of the coach. "The sergeant there is armed in much the same way, although he may only have his pistol in here. He has also seen plenty of action, if I don't miss my guess.

"As for myself, I am a fairly good shot with my handgun." He pulled his coat aside to show the polished butt of a gun strapped to his hip. "There are few men, or women for that matter, who do not go armed out here."

"I hadn't realized that." Esther let her voice trail off. She had read the descriptions of western life printed in English papers, of course, especially since deciding to accept Caleb's offer of marriage. She had assumed most of the accounts of Indians and bandits to be exaggerations of the truth to draw in more readers. Now it appeared that the reports could be true after all.

Soon after leaving the town behind them, the driver slowed the horses to a more sedate pace. Esther imagined the thundering departure was more due to the driver's sense of drama than any real need for haste. The pounding run and resulting cloud of dust would make an impression on anyone watching, she was sure. It certainly made an impression on her backside.

She eyed her sisters and wondered if their newly created bustles had cushioned them at all during those wild few minutes. Judging by the grimaces on their faces, they hadn't helped at all.

With Indians and bandits fresh in her mind, Esther recoiled and turned to the window at every shadow and every dip in the trail until the monotony of the landscape eased her mind. Surely, nothing harmful could hide in such flat land. Any attackers could be seen from miles away.

They stopped for dinner at in a tiny town, if it could be called such. In reality, it was no more than a collection of buildings beside a natural spring. Beside the stage station, was a corral with more of the sturdy horses that would replace the ones who had brought them the last twenty or so miles. A small trading post huddled on one side with darkened windows, their business done for the day.

Another building sat just beyond with brightly lit windows. A cowpony dozed at the hitching rail out front. A burst of music and feminine laughter spilled out into the darkening twilight as a man came staggering out still adjusting his hat. He freed the reins with one hand and attempted to mount his horse. It took him two tries before he swung up and tipped his hat toward the door he had just left.

Esther turned her gaze back to the stage station. She had never been so close to a 'house of ill repute' as her mother had called it. That was what happened to girls who had nowhere else to go. It redoubled her commitment to make sure her sisters were cared for. Nothing would be worse than to think of them in such a place.

Conversation around the table was general, with each of the young men in their company trying to outdo the other with stories they had heard or experienced. To see her sisters' laughing faces and bright eyes, the men were quite successful at impressing them. Only the muttonchopped man, Mr. Blake was the name he gave, focused entirely on his meal, his bag tucked securely between his feet. As for Esther, she ate quietly and watched the others.

If nothing else, the banter of the men had eased her sisters' grief. Esther had not seen them laugh like that since long before Father's final illness.

There were no overnight accommodations at this

stage stop, so the travelers would have to continue through the night. Somewhere ahead was a larger town where beds could be had for a few coins and the driver, as well as the passengers, would be able to grab a few hours of sleep before moving on.

The night was cold and clear with so many stars visible, it amazed Esther that it was the same sky she had viewed in England. Had there always been that many stars? She entertained herself trying to pick out the few constellations that she knew before uneasy sleep claimed her.

The bouncing of the stage through ruts and over rocks did not make for a smooth ride or a restful sleep regardless of what the Concord Company claimed. Esther climbed down stiffly when the stage reached its next destination. The stars still wheeled in their dance overhead, but she was too sore to try to admire them. At least here, they would be able to stretch out on a bed and get some real sleep before heading out again at dawn.

She had no idea how far they had come, or even what town they were in. All she cared about was lying down for one blissful hour. Charlotte and Isabella looked just as bedraggled as she felt.

No wonder traveling by stage was so much cheaper than the train.

The yawning stationmaster opened the door and waved them toward the back of the station. A curtained doorway guarded a row of narrow beds. Esther fixed her eyes on the rough blanket and made her feet take the few remaining steps between her and it. She lay down and closed her eyes with a sigh.

It seemed that no sooner had she closed her eyes than a rooster crowed, jolting her awake. She must have slept at least some because the gray light of predawn filtered between the gaps in the wall. She closed her eyes, revolting against the inevitable waking. The jangle of harness traces reminded her that if she didn't get up, she and her sisters would be stuck here until the next stage went through. That thought had even less appeal than getting up after only a few hours of sleep.

Esther sat up and looked over at her sisters still sprawled out, fully dressed, on the nearby beds.

Oh dear, this would not do at all.

With a grimace for the sore muscles, Esther forced herself to her feet. She stood there for a moment, waiting for the worst of the throbbing to pass. She probably should have removed her shoes the night before, but had no memory of lying down before she slept. She had the feeling that if she were to remove them now, they would not go back on.

She woke her sisters and they did what they could about their appearance with the help of the tepid water in the washbasin. It was amazing the difference a bit of water and a comb could do in the space of a few minutes. The rattle of plates was just beginning when the three women stepped from behind the blanket. The men around the table, their plates already piled high with bacon, eggs and biscuits, stood up and gazed with varying degrees of appreciation.

The men scrambled to pull out the sisters' chairs and seat them with all the ceremony of an English drawing room. Esther was surprised at their chivalry. She had come to believe that rough men from the dregs of society peopled the American West. She was finding instead that many of them were raised as well, or better than she had been with manners and education. So what drew them to this harsh land?

It seemed that eating was serious business here. All her attempts at small talk were brushed aside with short answers. She found out why when the stationmaster came in to announce that the horses were ready when they were. The driver shoveled an enormous forkful of eggs into his mouth, grabbed his hat and rifle, and went outside. The others followed suit leaving Esther and her sisters watching with plates still nearly half-full.

"Better hurry ladies or you'll be stuck here til the next stage and that doesn't come through for three days or more." The stationmaster chuckled as the women ate several fast bites.

One positive affect of wearing a corset, besides the obvious shape modifications, the tight stays left little room for large meals.

Esther braced herself for the lurching start, but couldn't stop the gasp created by muscles and body parts already sore from the day before. She tried to calculate how many more days of this they would have to tolerate before arriving in Santa Fe, but without knowing the stops, it was a futile effort.

The stage thumped through a large rut that jarred her insides. Maybe it would have been better to go hungry and stay on the train.

"Oh Esther, look." Isabella was pointing out a window. The sun was just peeking above the horizon and splashing the few clouds with a blaze of color. The colors shifted from red to pink to gold in the space of minutes, then the sun was fully up and beaming down on the world at its feet.

"Better keep an eye peeled for a storm later." The cheery cowboy's head hung upside down at the window.

"There is hardly a cloud in the sky, what makes you think there will be a storm?" Isabella asked with her most condescending tone.

The cowboy grinned at her, "Experience, pretty lady, experience." Then his face was gone.

Esther agreed with Isabella, a few lazy puffs of cloud did not signal a storm in her experience. Of course, this was a very different place than England where mists and fog drifted in from the sea nearly every day. This land seemed a world away from any water.

The land passed in the same monotonous manner as the day before. The coach paused briefly for lunch and a change of horses. When they started up again, the air felt heavy, even sluggish through the heat. Sweat traced a slick path down Esther's spine as she waved her fan at her face. Who would have believed this kind of smothering heat could follow the crisp chill of that morning?

With glazed eyes that struggled to stay open, Esther stared at a dark mass building on the horizon. The air was becoming too thick to breathe, laden with humidity and something else that left a strange taste at the back of her mouth.

A gust of wind brought a spattering of raindrops through the window. The soldier roused and slid the window beside him closed. Mr. Sheridan did the same for his window.

"Why not leave them open, a breeze would feel

wonderful in this heat." Charlotte leaned closer to her open window and drew in a deep breath. "With them closed, it will get stifling hot very quickly."

The driver cracked his whip sending the horses into a gallop even though there was no stop scheduled.

"What is going on?" Esther braced herself against the heaving seat. The thunder of a shotgun from the front of the stage was her answer. Several answering shots came from behind her. Bracing herself, she turned to peer out the narrow rear window. A dozen riders on painted horses pounded behind and to the sides of the coach. The riders were bare-chested and rode their horses without saddles.

"Indians." Esther turned back and cringed against the cushions. She felt the blood drain from her face. The men inside the coach all reached for their weapons and squinted through the closed windows.

"Why are they attacking now? Don't they know there is a storm coming . . . a big one?" Mr. Sheridan opened his window and took aim with his pistol.

The sound of the shot rang in her ears. Charlotte and Isabella, on either side of her cried out and buried their faces into her shoulders. She put an arm around each of them and held on tight. A warrior rode past aiming a rifle directly at her only to fling his hands out and fall to the ground as another shot blasted.

"Get on the floor!"

Esther didn't know for sure who shouted the command, but she was more than happy to pull her sisters down to the relative safety of the pitching floor.

Shots continued to sound from both inside and outside the thundering coach until she clapped her hands over her ears in a futile attempt to shut them out.

Finally, the coach slowed to a stop. The silence seemed to drag on for an eternity but it must have been only a minute or two. Esther drummed up the courage to glance up only to be blinded by a flash of brilliant light. The sulfur smell of brimstone filled the coach. The crash of thunder that followed was nearly as loud as the gunshots had been. The floodgates opened and rain fell in a torrent.

Esther eased back into her seat. Sargent Garrett leaned against the window holding his neckerchief to a patch of blood on his shoulder. Adam Sheridan seemed unharmed, peering out the window with his gun in his hand. Blake slouched against the cushions, his face drained of blood. His hand clenched around a small gun with a trickle of smoke rising from the barrel. She may have thought him dead but for the fact that his pale lips were moving in silent prayers.

"Why aren't we moving?" Charlotte climbed stiffly into her seat and stared with wide eyes at Adam.

"I fear something has happened to our driver. I will go check on him." Sargent Garrett moved to open the door.

"But you are wounded." Charlotte reached out to stop him but he just grinned.

"It is little more than a scratch, I have survived far worse. Besides, I need Adam to cover me just in case they aren't as gone as they seem."

"At least let me bandage it before you lose too much blood." Charlotte implored.

"Later, Charlie might need your services more than I do." Quicker than Esther would have expected of a wounded man, he was out the door and crouching beside the coach with only the top of his head visible. There was no movement beyond the curtain of rain and the Sargent moved forward to the driver's seat. The stage bounced a bit on its springs as he climbed up to the top.

A murmur of voices showed that someone at least was alive. Esther strained to make out some of the words but with no success. There was more bouncing just before Garrett's face appeared at the door he supported the driver using his good arm. She hurried to open the door and drew the soaked driver inside, laying him on the floor. His booted feet hung out the door, but they seemed to be out of the rain although Esther could see it streaming down not far away.

"The express rider is gone. Charlie says Curly fell off at some point but didn't think it wise to stop at the time. He managed to get us under an overhang that gives us some protection from the rain but we can't stay here long. These dry washes can fill up fast in this kind of rain. Once it slows down some, I'll drive toward the next station. You folks keep an eye out for our cowboy friend."

"I'm here." The young cowboy limped up, his normally cheery face tight with pain. He held one arm tight across his chest. "Blacked out for a few minutes after I fell. I woke in time to see them gather up their dead and head out. One of us got the war chief. Bad medicine. They won't be back until they have a ceremony to choose a new one."

"How do you know?" Mr. Blake spoke up for the first time in ages and everyone stared at him. "How do we know you aren't in cahoots with them redskins? Maybe you set them on us hoping to rob us." He wrapped his arms around his satchel and glared, his whiskered cheeks quivering. At least he didn't look dead anymore.

"You don't know what you are saying Mister." Adam said. "Curly here was up on top in full view of our attackers. He risked more than we did sitting inside the oak walls of this stage. I happen to know he wounded two of those Comanche braves. I would sooner question your motives than his."

"Mine? I don't know what you mean, sir." Blake raised his chin in what he obviously Charlotted was a dignified expression. To Esther, it seemed he was trying too hard.

"Enough of this." Garrett said. "This storm isn't going to get any better and we need to get these women to better shelter than we have here. Those indians might still come back."

Curly tipped his dripping hat to the women then climbed back to his perch at the top of the stage.

The rain did not let up for hours. Garrett kept the horses to a walk to protect the wounded men from excessive bumping. The road had become a swampy quagmire, washed away in places by rushing streams of water. The men took turns sheltering inside the stage. They tried to keep clear of the women at first, but it wasn't long before everyone was wet. The driver sat on the floor, his legs stretched out before him.

Isabella had done the best she could to bandage his wounds as well as those of Garrett and Curly, but she had only the most basic medical skills that she had learned from their mother. The read stain on the driver's chest continued to spread even after it was bandaged. His head had lolled back and now rested against the cushions. Esther couldn't tell if he was asleep or unconscious.

Her world had shrunk until it held only the gently rocking coach, the pouring torrent of rain and the occasional jingle of harness. The tedium of the journey had become a horrible nightmare, one she couldn't make herself wake from.

Charlotte sat in the seat opposite her. Her head lay against Adam's shoulder and she had tucked her feet up under her skirts. How she managed to sleep in that position with a corset on was more than Esther could fathom.

Isabella had finally given in to exhaustion and rested her head against the stagecoach wall. Her little sister looked pale and fragile after the eventful day. She had shown more courage and strength than Esther had known she possessed.

"You are lucky to have them." Adam spoke quietly into the gloom. The rain had persisted, but had slowed as evening approached. "They are good and selfless girls, a credit to their family."

Esther thought about their father, laughed at and ridiculed for most of his life. "The credit goes to themselves. We have no family to speak of."

"They have you." He smiled at her blush. "It is easy to tell that you have been the glue that holds them together. I think maybe you are lucky to have each other."

"We are. I can't imagine coming all this way, to a new land, a new life without them." Esther looked at the two faces she knew better than her own. "I Charlotte I have done the right thing in bringing them. I didn't believe it would be so dangerous."

"It isn't as dangerous as it once was." Adam glanced out the window. "The attack today was a rare thing, most of the tribes have settled on the reservations, even if they don't like it much. The buffalo are just about gone, taking with them the Indian way of life."

"Even so, this is a hard land and I don't know if I will be able to support them as they deserve. The man I am going to marry will welcome them, but he is not well off and will have little to offer." Esther looked at her hands folded in her lap. She was probably sharing too much, but the terror of the day and his helping to protect them had changed things.

"Perhaps they will marry. As beautiful as they are and pared with their sweet natures, I am sure there will be no end to suitors." Adam looked at Esther intently. "I would offer for Charlotte's hand this very day, but at the moment I have nothing to offer her. Not like she deserves."

Esther met his gaze and searched for some hint of insincerity. There was none.

"If you will wait until I have established myself a bit, I would like to come calling, once you are settled of course." Adam turned his head and looked down at the sleeping Charlotte. "I would do anything for her, anything to make her happy."

"I think you will." Esther smiled at him and marveled at how her opinion had changed over the course of a few days.

It was late when they arrived at the next station. A group of a dozen or so men milled their horses around as the stage horses limped in, heads hanging. One of the men rode up to the stage, peering through the windows before riding forward. Esther saw a glint of silver on his vest.

"Looks like you folks have had a tough time. We were just about to ride out after you." The man didn't wait for a reply. "There's vittles and coffee inside."

"We got a couple of wounded men. We had to leave the shotgun rider back where he fell. Charlie here is pretty bad." Adam leaned from the window. "Is there a doctor in town?"

"Yeah, young feller, but seems to know what he's doin'. Leave Charlie right where he is, we'll drive him right to Doc's place. You folks go on in and set a spell." The man paused and turned back to the stage. Esther saw the silver gleam on his chest again. This time she could see that it was a star shaped badge.

"By the way, any of you folks seen a man, graying hair with a leather satchel? He has them big bushy side-whiskers. Never could see the point of them myself, seems they would be near as hot as a full beard."

Esther glanced at the man sitting opposite her. His face had drained of all color and his eyes were wide with shock. His throat bobbed frantically as he tried to swallow.

Curly climbed down from the driver's seat to open the stage door. He scratched his cheeks where the stubble of whiskers was starting to show. He stared at Mr. Blake. "What's he wanted for?"

"Not entirely sure. Telegram came through a few hours ago sayin' he's wanted for questioning back in Dodge. Didn't seem like anything serious. You seen him?"

"Can't say." Curly blinked and looked back at the marshal. "I'll keep my eyes open though. Whiskers like that would stand out round here, that's for sure."

"Good enough, you folks have a good night, now." The marshal rode back to his men.

"Mister, I don't know who you are or what you've done, but you helped fight off that attack." Curly opened the door shielding it from the view of the mounded men. "This is your chance."

Blake, still pale as death, nodded and eased out of the stage, crouching to keep his head below the window level. Then he was gone, disappearing into the shadows.

Esther let her sisters precede her out of the stage, and then followed. She held Curly's hand as he helped her step down. Her sisters were already on the nearby boardwalk and heading toward the welcoming light glowing in the station windows. Before following them, she looked into the cowboy's merry face.

"Do you think that was wise?" She asked.

"What's that, ma'am?"

"Lying to the marshal. Mr. Blake has acted strangely for the whole journey. He probably broke the law, and you helped him escape. Why?" Esther peeked over her shoulder to make sure her sisters were still inside.

"I didn't lie." Curly's tone was cool. "I 'couldn't say' because my conscience told me that everyone deserves a second chance. Blake did help fight off the Indians and his actions are not those of a hardened criminal. If he is smart, he will turn himself in and return whatever is in that satchel. I think he's smart."

"And if he isn't?" Esther struggled to understand the cowboy's reasoning.

"Then it is on his conscience, not mine. I don't know about you, Miss, but I've needed a second chance or two in my life." Curly turned and walked away, shoulders straight and head high.

Esther followed slowly. He was right. Everyone deserves a second chance. Isn't that the reason that she and her sisters had come to this strange land? To start over where no one knew what they came from.

"Wake up, it's the mountains."

Esther was tempted to ignore her sister's plea. Isabella was always exclaiming over this natural beauty or that interesting rock, but something in her tone had Esther looking up. Off to the left, were the sun was descending toward the horizon, a mountain rose to dominate the landscape. There had been mountains in the distance for days, but although they had broken the monotony of the endless plains, they were far enough away to be featureless.

Two peaks, split from the rest of the range and towered over them. A forest of green trees carpeted its feet before giving way to bare rock still streaked with snow in some places. Esther caught her breath in awe. The clean smell of cedar rode the breeze, displacing that of sunbaked dust that had dogged their trail since leaving the train.

They stopped that night in their shadow. Esther and Isabella lingered beside the corral watching the last of the light fade from the summits long after the plains had been lost to shadow.

"The Spanish Peaks, some call them the twin peaks, although the eastern one is a bit smaller." Curly walked up and leaned against the corral. One booted foot rested on the bottom rail. For a long time, there was no sound other than the strident chirrup of some kind of insect and the occasional snort of a horse.

"It seems as though if I could climb to the very top, I would be among the stars." Isabella murmured. "I never imagined they would be so high."

"The Indians say there are many taller peaks, but none that extend out into the prairies quite so far." Curly glanced at Isabella's shining face. "I wouldn't want to see you among stars."

Isabella flushed and whirled toward him. "Why ever not? Who are to tell me what to do?"

The young cowboy didn't take offense to her tone; instead, he tipped back his wide brimmed hat and grinned. "I would never try to tell a filly like you what to do, but I bet if you were to climb up there with the stars, they would think you were one of their own and not let you come back down. That I'd surely hate to see."

Esther looked at her sister trying to judge Isabella's reaction to Curly's teasing. Most of the men they had met during their journey had seemed captivated by her beauty. They had done their best to flatter and charm her sister, but none had the creative flair of this young cowboy.

"Well, if they take me from way up there, you couldn't possibly see it anyway, so you're safe." Isabella kept her tone light, but Esther could see the blush that rose on her cheeks, even in the deepening twilight.

"Ah, but that is where you are wrong." His tone theatrical, Curly pulled his hat from his head showing the evidence of his name. He held the hat over his heart as he stared up at the silvery stars. "As the sailors' in days of old navigated by the constancy of the North Star, my heart will follow the most beautiful of stars to the world's end."

He shrugged and put the hat back on his head, "Until the clouds cover it up at least." And he ambled away.

Isabella stood still in shock and Esther couldn't stop the laughter that rolled up from her belly. Her sister was so accustomed to men who flattered her and hung on her every word she didn't know what to do with a man who teased her then walked away. After a haughty look at Esther, Isabella tossed her head and walked sedately to the hotel.

A week later, they rolled into Santa Fe.

Esther clenched her trembling hands on her lap as the stage thundered into town with its usual display. She kept her eyes glued to the floor, not daring to look out the window. After traveling thousands of miles across ocean, hills, plains and mountains, she had arrived at her destination. She was minutes away from meeting the man who would become her husband.

Oh dear.

A wave of nausea had her reaching for the door handle as soon as the stage rolled to a stop. Her feet were on the ground and she was leaning against the side of the stagecoach with her eyes closed fighting to keep her breakfast down. The midday sun burned her eyelids with relentless heat, but with none of the oppressive humidity of the Kansas plains.

A shadow blocked the sun's glare from her face. Esther opened her eyes and squinted at the man looming before her. The glare of the sun threw him into deep shadow and she could see nothing more than a black silhouette.

"You okay, Miss?" The man's voice was a bass rumble she could feel all the way to her toes. Before she could answer, another voice broke in.

"Hey, Boss, you wouldn't believe the trip I had." Curly stepped from the stage and held his hand out for Charlotte and Isabella to follow him. Adam was close behind.

"Indeed Curly. I asked you to hurry back and now here you are days late riding the stage. Why didn't you take the train?"

The young cowboy had the grace to look abashed. "Well, I missed the last train from Dodge that day so I took the stage thinkin' I would catch the train further down."

"And why didn't you?"

The words were stern, but Esther detected an underlying affection in the tone.

"Well, sir, there were these three beautiful ladies on the stage and I couldn't let them travel through Comanche territory without plenty of protection, now could I. You're the one that's been tellin' me that womenfolk are to be protected and cherished by menfolk, ain't that right."

"I haven't heard of the Comanche's bothering any stages lately, so I guess they were safe enough without you."

Esther couldn't remain quiet any longer. "Actually, sir, we were attacked and Mr. Curly was a big part in getting the stage safely through. He is a brave man and we are indebted to him."

The silhouetted man bowed in acknowledgement.

"I am glad if he was in anyway useful."

The man paused and looked at her. She couldn't see his eyes, but she felt the weight of his stare. His head turned as he took in her sisters on either side of her. Adam stood on one side of Charlotte and Isabella stood beside Curly with her hand tucked into the crook of his elbow. Apparently, she had gotten over her resentment of the young cowboy.

"I am sorry if I have offended any of you." He looked at Esther again and again she could feel the weight of his eyes. "Curly, would you introduce me to these fine ladies?"

There was a slight tremble to his voice, but no one else seemed to notice it.

"I would love to, Boss." He pulled away from Isabella a bit, but not far enough to lose contact with her hand, which he covered with his own. "This is Miss Isabella and her sisters Miss Charlotte and Miss Esther Westcott."

The man before them went still. The moment stretched until Esther's nerves frayed. "It is a pleasure to meet you, sir." She offered her hand and as he took it in his own, she dropped into a shallow curtsy then rose, expecting him to release her hand but he did not.

Instead, his hand trembled beneath her fingers. Oh dear.

She was about to tug it away, when he seemed to wake up from whatever dream he was in. Still holding her hand, he swept the wide brimmed hat from his head revealing deep brown hair and a strong, handsome face. His hazel eyes searched hers as he bowed and lifted her hand to his lips.

She had given up on wearing gloves since the heat

rendered them a soggy crumpled mess after a few hours in the stifling coach. Now, without that thin covering, she felt his lips brush across her knuckles. His breath tingled over her fingers, finding its way into every fold of skin. She shivered at the intimate contact.

Oh dear.

Curly cleared his throat, but his boss waved further introduction away. He stepped closer to Esther until their joined hands were trapped between them. She knew she should pull away, but staring into his intense eyes, she forgot why. Her chest burned with the breath that she had forgotten she held. She was afraid to let it out; afraid that this was a dream and breathing meant waking.

"Esther."

She shuddered at the way his voice caressed the name.

"At last. I'm Caleb."

She knew. Somehow, she knew that it was he.

At last.

Epilogue

Mrs. Caleb Jackson sat beside her new husband as he drove the wagon into the ranch yard. Behind them, in another wagon rode his ranch foreman, Curly with his new wife Isabella. Every few minutes, laughter or a bit of song would drift on the still morning air.

It was good to hear her sister singing and laughing again. Charlotte had stayed behind in Santa Fe. She had refused to wait for Adam's hotel to be a success before they married.

'Life is too short and uncertain to wait for happiness.' Charlotte had said. 'Sometimes you have to go find it.'

When had her younger sister grown so wise?

The ranch house appeared as Caleb drove the wagon around a stand of trees.

"I thought you said it was small?" Esther gasped with delight.

The house was two stories of the reddish stucco that was so common in the area. A wide porch wrapped around all four sides offering shelter from the blazing sun from any direction. From the shade of a nearby cluster of trees came a swarm of people. They reached the wagon and walked alongside toward the house, their smiles glowing out from dark skinned faces.

"It was small." Caleb nodded to the people walking beside them. "They are the reason it is so big now. I told them I was getting married and they came to help build it. They are our nearest neighbors, a village about half a day's ride to the north."

"It's wonderful." Esther smiled at the people around her as Caleb pulled the horses to a stop at the front door. "Thank you, all."

The faces around her brightened even more and at the edge of the crowd, a man with a stringed instrument she had never seen began to pluck a tune. Another man joined in with a horn and everyone began to clap and sing. A beautiful young woman with flashing eyes and dark hair began to dance, her full, brightly colored skirt swayed in time to the music.

"They have planned a fandango to celebrate your arrival." Caleb grinned. "It will likely go on for days."

"But they don't even know me." Esther exclaimed. A young man had joined the woman in the dance that seemed to include a great deal of foot stomping and hand clapping.

Some of the movements brought a blush to Esther's cheeks, but somehow when these people danced, the expressive movements didn't seem so scandalous. For them it was more of an illustration of the joy of living revealed on each of their faces. For the first time in her life, Esther understood that kind of joy and for a moment, she was tempted to join them.

Oh dear.

Late that night, Esther stood at the window. A cool breeze laced with the invigorating scent of pine caressed her face. A multitude of stars lit the sky and seemed to touch the timbered mountains that ringed her little valley. The haunting music of the villagers teased the edge of her senses, seeming to come from the land itself.

Everything was so different from what she had once known. It should feel strange, but it didn't. Caleb came up behind her and placed his warm hands on her shoulders. He placed a warm kiss on the back of her neck then gathered her back against his chest. His strong arms wrapped around her replacing the chill with soothing warmth.

"Are you thinking of home?" He murmured, his lips against her hair. "Are you sorry you came?"

Esther turned in the circle of his arms and looked up into his face. How could she love so strongly so soon?

"No, I'm not sorry." She laid her cheek on his chest and closed her eyes. "I am home."

Doreen Milstead

At last.

THE END

CPSIA information can be obtained
at www.ICGtesting.com
Printed in the USA
LVHW081301290321
682827LV00016B/318